Finding Baby Jesus
A Novella

Lynn Weathington

For my husband, Neil

and for all of those

who believe in Christmas miracles

Prologue

And it came to pass in those days, that there went out a decree from Caesar Augustus that all the world should be taxed. (And this taxing was first made when Cyrenius was governor of Syria.) And all went to be taxed, every one into his own city.

And Joseph also went up from Galilee, out of the city of Nazareth, into Judaea, unto the city of David, which is called Bethlehem; (because he was of the house and lineage of David:) To be taxed with Mary his espoused wife, being great with child.

And so it was, that, while they were there, the days were accomplished that she should be delivered. And she brought forth her firstborn son, and wrapped him in swaddling clothes, and laid him in a manger; because there was no room for them in the inn.

And there were in the same country shepherds abiding in the field, keeping watch over their flock by night. And, lo, the angel of the Lord came upon them, and the glory of the Lord shone round about them: and they were sore afraid. And the angel said unto them, "Fear not: for, behold, I bring you good tidings of great joy, which shall be to all people. For unto you is born this day in the city of David a Saviour, which is

Christ the Lord. And this shall be a sign unto you; Ye shall find the babe wrapped in swaddling clothes, lying in a manger."

And suddenly there was with the angel a multitude of the heavenly host praising God, and saying,

" Glory to God in the highest, and on earth peace, good will toward men."

And it came to pass, as the angels were gone away from them into heaven, the shepherds said one to another, Let us now go even unto Bethlehem, and see this thing which is come to pass, which the Lord hath made known unto us. And they came with haste, and found Mary, and Joseph, and the babe lying in a manger. And when they had seen it, they made known abroad the saying which was told them concerning this child. And all they that heard it wondered at those things which were told them by the shepherds. But Mary kept all these things, and pondered them in her heart. And the shepherds returned, glorifying and praising God for all the things that they had heard and seen, as it was told unto them.

from the Gospel of Luke, Chapter 2, verses 1-20

(King James Version)

Chapter 1

A Special Delivery

Suppose one of you has a hundred sheep and loses one of them. Doesn't he leave the ninety-nine in the open country and go after the lost sheep until he finds it? Luke 15:14

It was beginning to look a lot like Christmas, even though Leigh Mitchell Day's calendar showed late October and colorful autumn leaves swayed in the early afternoon sun. Busy municipal workers were wiring ornaments to the lampposts and replacing fall festival banners with those highlighting Butlerdale, Georgia's yuletide activities. Tonight was movie night at Moon and Stars, and Leigh finished changing the marquee to show the featured presentation. Her staff would show up in the evening to sell tickets, work the concession stand, and provide security. Her phone rang, and she returned inside to take the call from the university about an upcoming event.

The call was brief, and she sat sorting marquee letters for the next event. Glancing up from the desk, she raked her hand under her shoulder-length auburn hair as she rose to watch a delivery truck back into a vacant parking space out front.

Hugo Barnes, a burly man who delivered packages for most of his adult life, sighed as he opened the back of the vehicle to pull the theater's parcels. He noticed the jolly Christmas decorations and groaned. Hugo never enjoyed the holidays and dreaded the inevitable confrontations of frustrated customers who thought he could magically pull their precious cargo out of proverbial thin air. Grumbling to himself as he labored, he slid the final box out. It snagged on another package, tearing the packing tape and leaving a quarter-sized cavity. Shaking his head, he grabbed the box, turned it upside down to hide the hole, and placed it on his hand truck. Rolling the cargo past the ticket window, he met Leigh in her doorway. "Got a lot of boxes today for you, Leigh," he stated in a huff as she opened the door. "Just show me where you want 'em."

Once the grumpy courier dropped the parcels in the lobby and departed, Leigh began a hasty inventory, noting that most of them contained props and costumes for the upcoming production of "It's a Wonderful Life." There was one, however, that held something quite different.

After she and her husband, Jeremy, renovated the farmhouse where generations of her family lived, she desired to keep certain holiday customs alive. She remembered with fondness her mother setting up a tabletop nativity scene. Over the years, that well-used porcelain set served its purpose. Lately, Leigh wanted to begin new traditions, which included this set from Italy, manufactured by Fontanini™. Leigh smiled as she read the return address. She carefully sat the container inside her office to take home later, as she had an out-of-town appointment.

Driving toward Atlanta, she began to pray.

"Lord," she audibly spoke while maneuvering past the afternoon traffic jam around Butler High School. "Be with me today. You must be tired of me asking you over and over for a miracle." Struggling with her prayer, tears stung her eyes. Wiping her face with the back of her hand, she whispered, "Please help us."

Chapter 2

A Disappointing Appointment

Ask and it will be given to you; seek and you will find; knock and the door will be opened to you. For everyone who asks receives; the one who seeks finds; and to the one who knocks, the door will be opened. Matthew 7:7-8

The specialist's office contained the last patients of the day, and Leigh sat amongst them as she awaited her turn. Scattered magazines covered a table next to where she sat, but she couldn't get interested in any of them. They all seemed to feature new mothers beaming with delight at their newborns. Turning her attention away, she studied the remaining patients in the waiting room. A woman in her early forties sat in a corner reading a magazine and not making eye contact while a couple sat across from Leigh. The visibly pregnant wife held her husband's hand and wore a worried look. Watching them, Leigh wished she had persuaded Jeremy to accompany her instead of going solo. No one in the room had tolerance for small talk.

She and Jeremy had been together for almost ten years. They had fallen in love during their college days, and immediately after graduation, they married. In the early years of their union, there was no hurry for children. It was not until a few years ago, when she began to experience side effects from prescribed birth control and decided to discontinue them, that the couple realized their difficulty in conceiving a child.

Leigh discovered something amiss during a Labor Day trip to the beach. An early riser, she had gone for a walk along the seashore when abdominal pain interrupted her plans. Returning to the beach house where Jeremy still lay sleeping, the acute cramps had graduated to severe bleeding. Rushing to the bathroom as unbearable pain shot through her, she screamed in agony, sinking to the floor, too weak to stand. Jeremy, awakened by her cries, discovered her passed out on the tile floor, covered in blood. Panicked, he scooped her into his arms, carried her to his pickup truck, and sped to the nearest hospital. There, emergency room personnel concluded that Leigh had suffered a miscarriage. While she digested this news, Leigh received treatment that kept her hospitalized overnight. The next day, her attending physician was one of a parade of people who displayed sincere sympathy while assuring the young couple that countless others in this situation later gave birth to beautiful, healthy babies.

For the next few months, Leigh mourned the loss of the child. Only Jeremy witnessed the extent of her sadness since she had hidden the remorse from friends and family. Late at night, he would discover her out of bed and standing on the porch, gazing at a starry sky, her face streaked with trails of salty tears. Often, he would encircle her into his arms, where he would hold her as she cried. After weeks had passed, he did not know how to stop her tears, not understanding Leigh's guilt that she somehow caused the miscarriage.

Sensing Jeremy's cluelessness, Leigh found solace in the Scriptures, where she sought spiritual answers to conflicting emotions of anger, sadness, and grief that tugged at her heart. Hannah's story in the book of First Samuel gave Leigh hope for the future. She prayed nightly that God would answer her earnest prayers for a child. Leigh read the Bible many nights when she couldn't sleep while unconcerned and oblivious Jeremy dozed soundly beside her.

Two years later, life continued for Leigh and Jeremy as Leigh concentrated on keeping the theater alive and relevant with innovative shows and presentations. As a result of her tireless efforts, Moon and Stars survived and thrived. It was the place to gather for various live presentations and film festivals. Leigh spent long hours filling the theater's calendar with an array of events. An architect and contractor, Jeremy designed houses for a growing population that enjoyed the college town and its environs. His office occupied the upstairs loft of the theater building, although he rarely used it. His work took him to construction sites daily, and there was little time to sit behind a desk, although they did try to keep a weekly luncheon date if she wasn't dining with her closest friends, Beth, Abigail, and Amanda.

Leigh never gave up on her dream of becoming a mother. After fruitless months of no luck conceiving, Leigh consulted the local expert. Investigating options with her gynecologist, he recommended the fertility specialist she was visiting today. Leigh had already endured endless tests, from simple bloodwork to ultrasounds, x-rays, and even a laparoscopic procedure where all her reproductive organs received a thorough examination. It was there that the medical professionals discovered a resultant cause. Today's appointment was a continuation of her treatment, where the medical staff monitored oral hormone therapy, hoping they could overcome the condition and pave the way for conception.

A nurse came to the doorway and announced Leigh's name. As they exchanged pleasant conversation, she directed Leigh through the same routine they had been repeating for several months as specimens and bloodwork were gathered. Finally, everything culminated with the patient waiting in an examination room.

A few minutes later, Dr. John Freed, the physician Leigh entrusted to help with these obstacles, entered the exam room. A quirky man in his late fifties with thinning hair, a lanky build, and an eclectic wardrobe that always featured a bowtie and a colorful shirt underneath his lab coat, he was exhausted from dealing with emotional patients all afternoon. He was glad she was his last patient. "How are you feeling, Leigh?"

"Oh, I'm fine, thank you," she automatically shot back, reflecting her Southern upbringing.

He raised an eyebrow. "You realize you tell me that every time we meet." He sat on a stool to view test results on the laptop computer he had brought. "Are you resting better at night since we adjusted the prolactin?"

"Actually, no, but I think it's because I've got a lot going on at work. So I get in bed and think about everything I have to do the next day."

"You need a notepad and pen on your nightstand. There's no sense in allowing work to disrupt your downtime." He paused, and Leigh began to blush. She knew the next questions. "So, how are you and Jeremy getting along? Having regular intercourse?"

"Of course we are," she admitted, pulling out the small calendar she handed him. He had requested she keep a diary of her monthly cycle.

"Don't be embarrassed. This data's invaluable as we plot a course of treatment." He transferred information into the computer and returned the calendar to her. "Great job keeping track."

Leigh sighed. "Dr. Freed, we've been doing this for months. Am I making any progress?"

"All this takes time, Leigh. We know the problem is hormonal. Your body is producing all the right chemicals, but for some reason, when you ovulate, nothing happens. It's time for us to try something else. You may react to injection therapy."

"What does that entail?"

He opened a cabinet, pulling out a brochure he handed her. "You'll take a series of shots. These injections have been shown to increase the chances of pregnancy. My nurse will go over the process to show you how to self-administer. We'll monitor this closely, and you must follow the instructions. Risks are involved, but this may be your best chance to achieve a fertilized egg."

Leigh perked up but had concerns. "I've tried to be optimistic. How much does this increase our chances?"

"I've had numerous patients react positively to this type of therapy. If this doesn't succeed, there are other treatments we can consider. You've been pregnant before. While your body has healed from the trauma of your miscarriage, this is the next step."

Leigh had more questions about the therapy, and after their discussion, Dr. Freed departed. His nurse entered the exam room to give her vials and the syringes she would use, explaining how to give herself the shots. It was a lot to take in.

Later, sitting in her car, Leigh thumbed through the brochure. A young mother-to-be walked past her, smiling, radiant, and glowing, her baby belly covered by a cute maternity top. Leigh smiled back at her but could not push away the heavy hopelessness that she would never know that joy.

Leigh rested her head on the steering wheel, sadness overwhelming her. Pessimistic questions clouded her mind. Could she possibly pester God again with her prayers? Was He as weary as she was from hearing them? Could her heart take any more disappointment if this treatment didn't work, either?

Chapter 3

A Frustrated Freshman

Come to me, all you who are weary and burdened, and I will give you rest. Take my yoke upon you and learn from me, for I am gentle and humble in heart, and you will find rest for your souls. For my yoke is easy and my burden is light. Matthew 11:28-29

College freshman Lucy Grant despised her dorm room. It always seemed to reek of the sickeningly sweet perfume of her roommate, Ali Parker. While they rarely saw each other, as Lucy was an art major while Ali concentrated on early childhood education and socializing, it was almost too much to bear whenever Ali made a rare appearance, gushing with her latest escapades. The truth of the matter was that Ali thrived in college life while Lucy experienced homesickness.

This was Lucy's first time away from home. Besides the occasional marching band trip in high school, Lucy had never been away from her parents, Cory and Anna. It was something she had not anticipated in all the excitement over going to college and living on her own. Her childhood was marked by the countless times they moved due to Cory's work in medical equipment sales. Cory's promotion to management landed them in Athens, Georgia, near her grandparents, when she started eighth grade. That stability seemed to help a lifetime of shyness and allowed Lucy to emerge from her chrysalis to explore varied interests, including music, drama, and art. Her parents' protective nature undermined her flight toward independence, even though immaturity was to blame for most of her tentative missteps. She wasn't a bad teenager, but she was a terrible driver. Lucy lost her driving privileges after wrecking her Toyota Corolla three times in her senior year, ultimately totaling the car when she swerved to miss a squirrel, who survived.

Since she moved to Butlerdale and began classes at Butler University, Lucy noticed a subtle change in her parents. She could not determine what was going on. Whenever she talked with them, they seemed to be holding something back. She finally decided they were acting weird.

As she prepared to leave for class, she brushed her short, straight brown hair that matched her eyes. They were her favorite feature, although her self-confidence needed work. It did not help that she had a poor support system. In addition to the perplexing parents, she missed her high school friends, especially those from the marching band. After graduation, they scattered across the country to various colleges and universities. While they all promised to stay in touch, their communication dwindled to an occasional text or social media post. They, like Lucy, were experiencing their first taste of liberty.

Lucy bounded out the door to her favorite art class. She enjoyed painting and drawing, although her parents told her that mere talent and skill were not good enough attributes to parlay into a career and that she would need to switch her major to something marketable and stable. So far, she had delayed that change, and her parents, preoccupied with their weirdness, had said nothing.

Ahead of her, Hugo Barnes, still in a hurry delivering packages, hopped into his truck and started it up, forgetting he had left the back door open. As he sped away, he scattered packing peanuts and other debris from the cluttered floor of the truck. Lucy saw something small bounce out the back of the vehicle, and as she reached the curb, she noticed an item wrapped securely with bubble wrap held together by a tight rubber band. Picking up the pint-sized item, she hollered to the van driver to stop, but he had integrated into busy traffic. She studied it briefly before pocketing it and going on her way, knowing a vehicle would surely run over it if she left it in the street.

Sitting in class, the day's lesson consisted of charcoal sketches, and as usual, Lucy poured herself into the task. But, unfortunately, it always seemed that the class passed too quickly, and soon, her instructor gently announced their time was over for the day. While rambunctious and loud college kids pushed their way out of class,

Lucy remained to pack her supplies. She had thirty minutes to waste before her next class.

"Hey, you got a minute?"

Taken aback by a blonde student who approached her, she responded, "Um, are you talking to me?"

"Yeah, I just need a sec." She gestured toward the nearest table. "I'm Claire. My dorm room was damaged this week in a flood. Burst water pipe. My roommates have found a new place off campus, but they need four people to make the rent."

"What does that have to do with me?" Lucy looked puzzled.

"Ali Parker's your roommate, right? She wants to move into the house, but that leaves me homeless."

"Oh, um, okay," Lucy didn't know how to respond. She figured there were rules about changing roommates after a semester started.

"Ali loves to party. Heck, I used to party a lot when I first got here! I'm a junior, and it's been a distraction with the non-stop partying this semester. I'm hoping to find a quieter place."

"Well, living with me qualifies," Lucy quipped. "I'm not much for partying. I won't mind the switch if it's okay with the housing department."

"Done that. It won't be a problem." Claire's face lit up with a spectacular smile. She was glad she approached Lucy.

As they departed the classroom, Claire inquired of Lucy yet another question. "Hey, do you have classes tonight?"

"I'm done at five. Why?"

"Have you been to CCF? They always have great food, and the music and people are awesome. You can come with me tonight if you'd like."

"What's CCF?"

"It's the Christian Campus Fellowship." Claire paused when she saw a subtle scowl on Leigh's face. She saw this a lot when inviting students to the campus ministry. "Hey, don't worry. It's a free meal, no pressure. You get cookies, we've got a band, sometimes there's prizes."

Lucy's parents never attended church. The only time she ever remembered going was with her grandparents, and while she enjoyed parts of the services she attended, the visits were so infrequent that she didn't consider it a necessity. She believed there was a God and had a rudimentary idea of who Jesus was, but church wasn't a priority. She immediately gave an excuse to Claire.

"Um, I'm not really religious."

"That's okay. You don't have to be. As I said, it's a free meal. You gotta eat somewhere, right?"

"Lemme think about it," she said as she walked away, her mind already made up not to attend.

Chapter 4
Hungry College Students

*"Blessed are those who hunger and thirst for righteousness,
for they shall be satisfied."* Matthew 5:6

Claire's invitation to CCF confused Lucy. After finishing classes for the day, Lucy thought again of how lonely she had been these last few months. It might be good to get out just once. Since this was a religious organization, she wouldn't be pressured to drink or do things she would regret later. If she didn't like it, she could always tell Claire she didn't want to attend if she asked her in the future.

Ultimately, Lucy decided to dine at the student center. It was across the street from the humanities building she just left, and enticing scents lured her there.

After ordering her meal, she pulled a debit card from her wallet to pay. The kiosk kept showing "declined" after numerous swipes. Impatient students began lining up behind her.

The cashier behind the counter tried to help. "Do you have another card?"

"Um, no, this one usually works. I don't understand what's going on."

The clerk looked at the screen and assessed the situation. "Looks like you're not eating here tonight. Sorry." Unsympathetic, the clerk canceled Lucy's order and asked who was next.

Mortified, Lucy's face turned crimson as she retreated. As she passed, she felt the other students' stares and imagined them judging her. How did she get into this hot mess? Finding an empty table, she pulled out her phone to text her dad, but he didn't respond. Realizing that her father had not made his usual transfer, she weighed her options. She decided a free meal was better than no meal.

Twilight had begun to envelop the day, so Lucy quickened her pace as she left the student center. Stopping to ask a female police officer for directions, she pointed her toward a tree-lined avenue just north of the main campus. The CCF house sat in a row of similar buildings that housed a variety of religious organizations. When she arrived, she immediately saw Claire.

Happy to see Lucy, Claire greeted her. "I'm glad you came," she encouraged while completing a name badge for Lucy to wear. "Doesn't dinner smell great? It's Italian night!"

Claire stayed by Lucy's side as she introduced her to countless people. Initially overwhelmed by the number of students, Lucy nodded and mumbled through the introductions. Someone encouraged her to prepare a plate of homemade spaghetti and Caesar salad. A local church provided the meal, and since it was a pleasant night, everyone ate outside at picnic tables. She and Claire sat with a couple of young men whom Lucy discovered later played in the house band. There, Claire revealed that she was a music major concentrating on piano. Lucy was drawn to one of the guys who also majored in music. He introduced himself as Tristian, and she immediately enjoyed his quirky sense of humor. Lucy returned for seconds, and one of the servers mentioned a to-go plate.

When the programming began, the house band played unfamiliar songs that Lucy did not recognize. There was no "Amazing Grace" or any hymns from the church back home. How could this be? What was the word she struggled to remember... sacrilegious? Her grandmother once used the word to describe a similar group who visited her church. Yet...She enjoyed the beat and wailing guitar solos. It reminded her of summer nights in Athens when she and her friends would enjoy live music in their hometown. After the band finished their set, an enthusiastic campus minister led a goofy trivia game. She didn't know many answers until he asked, "How many paintings did Vincent Van Gogh sell during his lifetime?"

No one knew the correct answer, so she announced, "Um, one, the 'Red Vineyard at Arles.'"

"We have a winner!" He picked up a bag of cookies and tossed them to Lucy. She beamed as if she had won the lottery.

The trivia segued into a devotional talk about the pressures of campus life and the various temptations students encountered. He addressed various issues, including drug and alcohol abuse, partying, promiscuity, and cheating. His answers to these challenges seemed to always come from the Bible, which he kept quoting. Unlike her grandmother's minister, who spoke too long, his talk only lasted a few minutes before the band returned to the stage. Once the music ended, the students continued socializing, unhurried in leaving.

Leather books were stacked on a table, and curious, Lucy picked up one with a teal cover embossed with flowers and a butterfly. When she flipped it open, she discovered it was a Bible. Suddenly, she knocked over the display, and Bibles scattered across the table.

"Do you need a Bible?" The campus minister asked, approaching her.

"Um, no," Lucy stammered as she looked for an escape route.

He helped restack them. "Oh, they're free. Take it if you need one."

"Okay. Um, thanks." She slipped it into her backpack.

"Is this your first time at CCF?"

"Um, yes. Claire invited me."

"I'm glad you're here. Come back anytime!" He smiled before turning away to greet other students.

It was almost ten o'clock when Lucy returned to her dorm. Ali was already packing boxes for her move, and Lucy almost didn't mind the perfume since she knew Ali wouldn't be there much longer. They were strangers, and it was odd that they had shared the same space for two months but knew so little about each other. In contrast, Lucy had learned more about Claire, her boyfriend Tate, Tristian, and other newfound acquaintances in mere hours. Confused about a religion that came with a rock beat, she decided to keep an open mind. At least she could go there to get food. And cookies.

When she checked her phone, her dad had not texted her back. It wasn't unusual for him to go off the radar when he entertained clients. She would ask her mom in the morning about making the transfer.

As she readied for bed, she reached into her jacket pocket to extract her keys, and when she did, she found the little package she picked up earlier. She removed a rubber band and started undoing the item from its tight wrapping. It was a miniature figurine of a baby wearing a white onesie and lying in a basket. Admiring it momentarily, she smiled as she sat it on her desk, glad she had saved it from the street.

Chapter 5

An Absent Husband

And as for you, brothers and sisters, never tire of doing what is good. 2 Thessalonians 3:13

Jeremy was already there when Leigh got home from her doctor's appointment. She couldn't enter the garage because he had pulled a large roll-around toolbox and workbench into her parking space, so she left her car in the driveway.

"What's going on?" Leigh gestured toward a cordless nail gun and a pile of tarps.

"There was a tornado outbreak in Alabama today. Our emergency response team is leaving at first light." He resumed filling a stainless steel toolbox with essentials.

Leigh sighed. She wanted to share a quiet evening with her husband while she enlightened him about the new therapy she would be starting.

"Have you packed?"

"Not yet."

"I'll go do it." Aggravated, she entered the house and headed for their bedroom, pulling clothing from his dresser as she packed a duffle bag. She was familiar with this drill. One of the things that endeared Jeremy to her heart and simultaneously drove her crazy was his ability to drop everything to help someone in need. Her uncle, Mason Young, would partner with him in the morning to rendezvous with the other crew members as they took a caravan of travel trailers to the affected area.

After a brief dinner of microwaved leftovers, a flurry of phone calls kept Jeremy tied up all evening as he made arrangements with local subcontractors about his current construction projects. Exhausted from battling Atlanta traffic and still perturbed about Jeremy's imminent departure, she went to bed. She had dozed for a few hours when she felt Jeremy turning back the covers.

"I'm not asleep," she denied, rolling over to face him.

"You're so irresistible when you tell me little lies." He kissed her tenderly.

She yawned. "Did you get everything done so you can leave?"

"I've got one more thing to take care of." She recognized that mischievous grin as he began caressing her. She responded to his touch with playfulness and complete submission.

Snuggling next to him afterward, his warmth spreading to her as a light snore emulated from his lips, Leigh closed her eyes. She prayed that God would keep him and the other volunteers safe from harm, finishing with a short wish for conception. It never hurt to ask!

Leigh rose earlier than Jeremy the next morning to prepare breakfast. When he came into their kitchen to pour a cup of coffee, he wrapped his arms around Leigh from behind and rested his chin upon her shoulder. "Good morning," he murmured in her ear as she prepared his favorite, a southwestern omelet. "You didn't have to get up this early."

"I couldn't sleep. You know me," she responded while turning the almost-ready omelet in the skillet. "I sleep so seldom anyway."

"You never did tell me about your visit with Dr. Freed yesterday."

"No, I didn't. Pretty much the same thing. He wants me to try some different hormones. Nothing that can't wait until you get back home."

"Something to look forward to," he teased, kissing her neck.

They enjoyed breakfast as Jeremy outlined where he was heading. Leigh took it all in, remembering the small towns affected by the storm and glad that the team could assemble and organize so swiftly. It was six-thirty when Leigh's uncle drove up in his RV.

Mason Young pastored the local Christian church, but it was his passion to lead the emergency response team whenever needed. He would take a few days away from his church duties to organize their command center, where the other volunteers would remain to integrate with other groups. Because of Mason's leadership, the volunteers he assembled possessed various talents, and Jeremy usually served as operations coordinator. Before she took ownership of the theater, Leigh had accompanied the group to prepare meals and do odd jobs, but lately, she had remained at home as the theater consumed more and more of her time.

Waving toward Mason as he parked the RV, Jeremy carried his heavy toolbox toward the back of the vehicle. When he returned to the garage to gather his duffle bag and rain gear, he saw Leigh standing in the shadows with her arms folded. "Listen, I don't know how long I'll be, but don't worry. We'll be back before the holidays."

"Take whatever time you need," she responded. "Just be careful."

He placed the items inside the cargo hold, closed the hatch, and locked it. Opening the passenger door, he stopped short of entering the vehicle. "Hey, Mason, I forgot something in the house. I'll be right back."

Dashing into the garage, Jeremy propelled Leigh into the kitchen and shut the door. He took her into his arms and kissed her with a fervency that never diminished in all the years they had known each other. "I love you. Thank you for always understanding this is a part of me."

The extra hormones made her more tearful than usual. "I love you, too."

Leigh accompanied Jeremy to the RV. She didn't want to appear clingy, so she walked toward the driver's side to say hello to her uncle. Jeremy climbed into the camper and waved to her as the vehicle rolled away.

Chapter 6
A Helpful Assistant

Whatever you do, work at it with all your heart, as working for the Lord. Colossians 3:23

Lucy's social life took a turn for the better after Claire moved in with her. Claire knew everyone and gave her a tour of the thriving college town. It was a windy November day when Claire introduced Lucy to Beth Young.

Entering Magnolia Studios on the square, the two college students met Beth, an attractive woman around thirty with curly copper hair, a spectacular smile, and emerald eyes hiding behind wire-rimmed glasses. She took an immediate interest in Claire's new friend. "So glad to meet you, Lucy. Would you both like a bottle of water? It's so blustery and dry today."

Beth offered them a seat in a small waiting area. "I've taught Claire piano for about five years now. She's one of my favorite students!"

"I am? I didn't know that!" Claire shook her blonde hair and grinned. "Is that why you hired me to work for you this Christmas?"

"You'd badgered me for weeks!" Beth equaled Claire's amusing banter. "You wore me down!"

"I told Lucy that the downtown businesses sometimes offer seasonal employment during the holidays. Do you know anyone who's hiring?"

Beth wrinkled her brow as she ran her hand absently through her hair. "Let's see...someone mentioned needing help the other day." Peering out the window, she suddenly remembered. "Leigh Day needs someone to design and paint background sets for one of the Christmas productions at the Moon and Stars Theater."

Lucy beamed. "I'm an art major," she stated with quiet enthusiasm. "Maybe I can help."

"I'm certain Leigh's in her office. She'll be happy to see you both."

They ran across the busy square to the theater building. Looking up, Lucy paused to admire the art deco design of the decades-old two-story building. She wondered what it looked like at night. Claire pointed to a door to the left of the foyer. An old-fashioned doorbell jingled in greeting as they entered the office. No one was sitting at the desk, but they heard one side of a heated conversation.

Leigh's voice resonated with anger. "You didn't hear me. I said I'd get the sets done. There's no need to raise your voice. Call me next week, and I'll give you a progress report!" She stomped back into the office area. Realizing Claire and her friend overheard her argument with an impossible play producer, she began to smooth over the situation.

"Sorry about that, Claire. I didn't realize I had company." She turned toward Lucy. "Hi, I'm Leigh. Welcome to the house of chaos."

"I'm Lucy Grant. Um, Beth Young said you might need help with your Christmas show."

"I'm looking for someone to paint and decorate the sets. Do you have any experience?"

"I painted sets in high school for plays? I like costumes, props, painting sets, um, doing stuff behind the scenes."

Leigh beamed. "Great! We're behind on the production because the sets aren't ready. I'd like a reference and maybe samples of your work. Is that okay? If it all works out, maybe you can start this week?"

After completing an application, providing contact information, and texting photos, Lucy found Claire, who had walked out to the foyer to text her boyfriend.

"How'd it go?"

"Leigh's going to check my references and get back to me."

Returning to Claire's car, Claire pointed out a loft suite photography studio displaying a "help wanted" sign in the window. They ascended the stairs to arrive at a door that read "Amanda Rivers Photography" etched in the glass. They found Amanda, the photographer, shooting a formal Christmas portrait of a local family inside the sparsely furnished loft. Waiting in a sitting area consisting of a few chairs and a coffee table, Lucy noticed stunning nature scenes on the walls, and she became engrossed in them, noting the photographer's unique perspective.

Watching Amanda work, she admired how she made the family feel at ease. With long red hair pinned loosely atop her head, she moved gracefully and catlike as she stopped from time to time to adjust equipment to capture her subjects in the best light possible.

When the session ended, the mother gathered coats and bundled her children. The brother and sister started a squabble with each other before their father hushed them, and they left the loft arguing about visiting the ice cream parlor. Amanda switched off the lights of the Christmas set to greet the newcomers. Carrying a well-used Nikon professional camera, she changed lenses before setting the equipment on a cluttered worktable. "Hi, Claire," Amanda greeted as she hugged her young friend. "It's so good to see you."

"Hey Amanda," Claire said. "This is my new roommate, Lucy Grant."

Amanda smiled. "So glad to meet you. So, what brings the two of you here today?"

"Lucy's looking for a job," Claire explained. "We saw your sign in the window."

Amanda's face lighted up at the prospect of hiring a college student. "Do you have any experience in photography?"

"Um, I'm an art major," she revealed. "I'm taking a basic photography class. It's really interesting." Gesturing toward the canvases decorating the walls, she added, "Your stuff is gorgeous."

"Thanks!" Amanda reached up to adjust her hair clasp. "I started photography around your age. I'm shooting a lot of families for their annual holiday cards. Having an assistant who could help speed things along would be nice. Who is your photography professor?"

"Dr. Daniels."

"She was one of my professors, too," Amanda disclosed. "She's tough but fair. I'll call her tonight and get back to you."

Lucy brightened at the offer. "Thanks so much! I really appreciate it!"

Lucy and Claire left the photography studio, found their way to the gazebo in the center of the town square, and sat on a bench. "So, which one of the jobs do you hope to land?"

"Oh, they both seem cool. I applied at a couple of places at the mall, but no one called me back." She paused as something clicked. "Claire, are all the downtown shops run by redheads?"

Claire giggled. "It seems like it, but Leigh, Beth, and Amanda are all cousins."

"Wow. They all seem so successful."

"They're all friends of my Aunt Abigail, who doesn't have red hair. Amanda's parents own the farm store; after college, she set up shop upstairs. She's one of the best portrait photographers around. Leigh and her husband, Jeremy, own the theater building. He's an architect and local contractor. Beth's pretty quiet but ultra-talented. Her dad's the pastor at First Christian Church. They've done a lot for the downtown area. I've lived here all my life and love this place."

That evening, Lucy received a phone call from Amanda Rivers. "Hey, Lucy, I talked with Dr. Daniels, and she said you had a lot of potential. I've got a big shoot next Monday, so I'll see you around two."

At one-thirty the next Monday, Lucy finished her art class and headed to the bus stop that took her to the downtown square. Fifteen minutes later, she walked up the steps to the photography studio. Amanda put her to work packing tripods and lighting equipment as the duo departed for a holiday shoot at a physician's office. Amanda photographed the large staff of professionals and their families for their annual Christmas cards. Nervous, Lucy knocked over an umbrella lamp, tripped over an extension cord, and spilled a box of AA lithium batteries. Amanda didn't notice as she wove magic around her subjects, charming squirmy, uncooperative children and achieving happy expressions in the final images. Instinctively, Lucy calmed down and managed not to break anything, although finding all those batteries took a while. Once finished, they returned to the studio, where Amanda showed Leigh how to edit the digital images.

That evening, Amanda drove Lucy back to her dorm. "Did I do okay today?" Lucy asked as they rode along holiday-decorated streets before driving to the residence hall.

"Yeah, you did fine. I'll call when I need you again, okay?"

Lucy hummed "Jingle Bells" as she ascended steps to her room. Claire heard her as she unlocked the door. "Hey you," Claire said. "How'd it go?"

"Um, I messed up a little, but Amanda said I did fine."

Claire pulled on a denim jacket.

"Where are you going?"

"Over to the CCF house to practice. I'm playing keyboards for the band this week. You wanna come?"

Leigh put back on her jacket, grabbed a protein bar, and followed Claire out the door.

Chapter 7

A Busy Bee

Sow your seed in the morning, and at evening let your hands not be idle, for you do not know which will succeed, whether this or that, or whether both will do equally well.
Ecclesiastes 11:6

The next morning, Lucy caught the downtown bus after her English literature class to ride to Moon and Stars to begin working on the theater sets for "It's a Wonderful Life." Leigh called Lucy that morning to see if she could come to work for her. Greeting the new employee with a cup of cappuccino, Leigh prepared her drink as she explained the concept of the play based on the classic movie. The sets switched quickly from one scene to another as it chronicled the life of beleaguered banker George Bailey. The production company had ideas for various backdrops, but it would be Lucy's task to bring these to life. They included the iconic streetscape of Bedford Falls, with an almost identical canvas depicting the alternative reality town of Pottersville. One of the most interesting backgrounds employed twinkling lights that stood in for the Christmas Eve sky for most of the "outdoor" scenes. Lucy would prepare ten sets before the last week of rehearsals, which coincided with the first week of December. It was a daunting task, but Lucy loved the work. By six o'clock that evening, she had finished the night sky panel. She was already measuring and marking where she would insert LED bulbs the next day, using a diagram that accompanied the production manager's instructions.

Impressed by Lucy's work ethic, Leigh walked into the workshop and saw Lucy wearing wireless earbuds, humming happily to her personal music as she marked the back of the canvas with a marker. It was so refreshing to see such enthusiasm, and for a few minutes, Leigh watched as she thought Lucy surely had to be tired after such a long day. Startled by Leigh, Lucy turned over a glass jar that held several paintbrushes. Dark water spilled across a work table, and Leigh vigorously mopped the mess with a well-stained towel.

"I can't believe you've already finished one of the panels!" Leigh exclaimed as she examined Lucy's efforts. "This looks great! I love the graduated colors from black to midnight blue and the slight wisps of clouds. This will look stunning once the lights are installed."

Beaming, Lucy relished Leigh's praise. "I think I'm done," she began wiping her hands on the towel. "Where can I put this?"

Leigh pointed toward a small closet with louvered doors. "We have a washer and dryer in there. Just put it in one of the hampers, and I'll do the laundry later. You would be amazed at how much we have to keep clean here."

Lucy washed her hands, hung up her smock, and picked up her jacket and purse. "I got classes tomorrow morning, but I can come back at two."

"Perfect!" Leigh's smile turned serious. "Hey, I know you're working for Amanda, too. Let me know if this is too much for you."

"It's good. I like being busy. Amanda won't need me again until this weekend. Before this week, I had little to do except go to classes. I now have things to do in my free time, thanks to Claire."

The pair turned off the backstage lights. The old theater building's wooden floors creaked as their footsteps echoed in the empty foyer. "How old is this place?" Lucy inquired, realizing again the age of the well-maintained and fully restored structure.

"It was originally built in the 1930s as the Western theater, the first movie theater in Butlerdale. When the mall multiplex theater was built on the other side of town, it closed and sat idle for decades. A few years ago, the downtown merchants' association realized it was about to be razed by an out-of-town apartment developer, so my husband and I decided to make an offer on the building. It took a while to bring it back to life. Jeremy brought it up to local codes, and I've secured several grants to keep it within the parameters of historical significance in its restoration. Since the town doesn't have a municipal auditorium, we offer it to the community for various productions. The high school jazz band will present a concert tomorrow night, and this weekend, we have a ballet troupe from the university scheduled to perform." Leigh retrieved a sweater and purse from her office before locking the door. "We show a classic movie every week for 'Stars over Butlerdale.' I'm ecstatic that the theater is still relevant. So many of these structures no longer exist or have a purpose." Setting the alarm system, they exited the building.

"Why did you rename the theater?" Lucy gestured toward the Moon and Stars logo above the neon-lighted marquee with chasing lights.

"I love old movies," Leigh explained. "It comes from a line from a Bette Davis film 'Now Voyager,' which was 'don't let us ask for the moon when we have the stars.'"

Lucy didn't know who Bette Davis was.

"It was the only thing I fought for during the historic preservation. It took some doing, and I wore the committee down. They agreed I could call it anything I wanted."

Enticing smells wafted from the nearby restaurants, and Lucy's stomach growled. Realizing she had little cash, she dismissed her hunger, but Leigh read her mind. "I'm starving! Let's have dinner before you go back to campus. It's the least I can do."

Entering a nearby Chinese restaurant, they were ushered to an empty table as a young waitress took their order. Soon, they were enjoying grilled vegetables with teriyaki chicken and rice. The diminutive eatery soon filled with diners.

"You mentioned your husband earlier. Um, you both own the theater?"

"That's right. Jeremy's out of town for the next few weeks. He works with the local emergency response team through our church. Did you hear about the tornadoes in Alabama? He's helping with storm cleanup."

Leigh was glad that she suggested dining with Lucy. It beat going home to an empty house, allowing her to learn more about her new employee. "So, tell me a little about yourself, Lucy. Where did you grow up? What do you like to do?"

Warming to Leigh's gentle persona, she shared a brief life story. "I'm from Athens. I wanted to go to SCAD, but my mom and dad wanted me someplace more traditional, so here I am."

"I got my degree at Butler U, and Amanda's an alum, too. The art department isn't as well known as SCAD, but you'll get a solid education. Our nightlife in Butlerdale isn't as lively as Savannah's, but we have many things to do here."

"I took most of my core classes online in high school, so I'll be a sophomore next semester. I'd like to do something with my degree other than teach. That's what my parents seem to want me to do."

Impressed by Lucy's drive and determination, Leigh kept going. "Your degree isn't just for teaching. So, how often do you see your parents?"

"They haven't been back since moving me in, but I talk with them daily. They'll probably come get me for Thanksgiving."

Their server appeared with a check and two fortune cookies. After paying, Leigh offered one of the cookies to Lucy before opening hers.

"I cannot help you, for I am just a cookie," Leigh read, laughing at the offbeat humor.

Lucy opened hers and found the following message. She scanned it silently before repeating out loud, "Don't be afraid to try something new."

"I think yours is better," Leigh acknowledged. "I know you're experiencing many fresh and exciting things these days."

Bright lights illuminated the square as they walked along the sidewalk toward the municipal parking deck directly behind Rivers Seed and Feed. A covered bus stop where Lucy would wait for transportation sat immediately across the street, and she turned to thank Leigh for the meal.

"Where are you parked, Lucy? I'll be glad to walk you to your car."

"Oh, I took the bus. I don't have a car. It's too cold to ride my bike at night."

"The bus to the university doesn't run the downtown route at night as often as during the day. It might be an hour before it comes by. Listen, I'll gladly drive you back to your dorm."

Lucy protested, but Leigh's SUV was parked nearby. She clicked her key fob, and the lights came on. "Hop in. It's on my way home."

After Leigh dropped off Lucy on campus and started home, her heart began to yearn for Jeremy. He had been gone only a few days, but it felt much longer. While she would try to call him once she got home, she thought again about how God may have introduced Lucy into her life because the bright college student needed a place to showcase her talents. Her presence was a welcome distraction to her introspective thoughts.

Chapter 8

A Devastated Community

"'For I was hungry and you gave me something to eat, I was thirsty and you gave me something to drink, I was a stranger and you invited me in, I needed clothes and you clothed me, I was sick and you looked after me, I was in prison and you came to visit me.' "Then the righteous will answer him, 'Lord, when did we see you hungry and feed you, or thirsty and give you something to drink? When did we see you a stranger and invite you in, or needing clothes and clothe you? When did we see you sick or in prison and go to visit you?' "The King will reply, 'Truly

I tell you, whatever you did for one of the least of these brothers and sisters of mine, you did for me.'" Matthew 25:35-40

After another grueling fourteen-hour shift, Jeremy sat on a camp stool outside Mason Young's RV. In all the years of his responding to natural disasters, this one had been the worst he had ever seen. Closing his eyes, he could still see the devastation, house after house, neighborhood after neighborhood. The tornadoes had ripped a two-mile-wide swath over fifty miles, and there were places where nothing remained except concrete foundations. When he wasn't using a chainsaw to cut away trees on top of homes, he was climbing on damaged roofs, helping to secure tarps. Even though he was in fine physical form and was used to construction sites, the sheer volume of work he and his crew did just wore him out.

The smell of fresh sap permeated the air. In the distance, the whine of power saws continued, although, with nightfall, most of the volunteers ceased operation because of darkness and fatigue. Too tired to move, Jeremy sat, contemplating his evening and waiting for Mason to return to the encampment, as they had separated within the last couple of hours. Removing his hard hat, he laid it on a table and brushed sawdust from his wavy black hair. Rubbing a stubble-covered chin, he realized he had not shaved since he left Butlerdale a week ago. Smiling, he thought of Leigh and wondered what she would think of his disheveled, unkempt look. He imagined her offering to draw him a nice, hot bath and the thought of her sponging his shoulders, his aching back. Nirvana!

Had Leigh not taken on the theater, she would be there alongside him as she had done earlier in their marriage. Shifting to the present, it wasn't that he resented their buying and meticulously restoring the old Western Theater and transforming it to Moon and Stars, but he wondered how Leigh would keep up her own demanding schedule once a child came into their lives. The nightmare of her miscarriage still haunted him, and even though he supported her fertility treatments, the last thing he wanted was to jeopardize Leigh's health in their quest to procreate. He wasn't sure he was father material, but he didn't dare squash her dreams.

His thoughts turned to children, and he witnessed so many displaced by the storm, lives turned irrevocably upside down. He and Mason ministered to many families this week, people who held onto one another in closets and bathrooms and basements as they watched with horror their houses torn away from their foundations and blown completely away. It was a miracle of God that no one had died during the catastrophic storm, although during their initial sweep of neighborhoods, they aided countless survivors who were still trapped in the remaining wreckage of their homes. Everyone had a harrowing tale to tell.

Since it had been a week, the relief crews began to encounter the difficulties of people on their own, without electricity, running water, and heat sources. These survivors now hunkered down in their damaged residences, reduced to foraging for basic necessities. Jeremy was reminded of Jesus in Matthew's gospel as he endorsed giving a cup of cold water to those in need. He was so grateful for the truckloads of bottled water that had begun to arrive, the answer to a nationwide appeal for help and now one of the most treasured commodities.

Eli Jones drove up in his pickup truck to drop off Mason. A giant of a man with short-cropped blonde hair, Eli was a second-generation cabinet maker. Mustering his last bit of energy, Jeremy rose to help the pair unload some supplies they had picked up at the command center. Turning to light a propane camp stove, Jeremy prepared canned chili as their dinner as Eli and Mason shared a recap of their day's adventures.

"Eli and I visited a church about a mile from here," Mason incanted, "nothing's left of the exterior brick walls, the steeple, and the roof, but the interior's still intact. The pews, the pulpit, the communion table, and the baptistery are still there. Even the hymnals are still in place in their racks. The children's area in a separate building is relatively untouched. Church leadership said after an initial inspection that they could resume preschool classes once the electricity is restored."

"That would be a good thing, a place where some of the children could go," Eli replied optimistically. "I was at the local elementary school yesterday, and except for debris all over campus, classes can continue there, too. When we left, refugees were coming in to spend the night. We passed out blankets and pillows for everyone wanting to stay there."

Eli turned to Jeremy. "You talked to Leigh?"

"I was planning on calling her tonight. The cell tower at the back of the campground seems to be working again, and I know she's antsy to hear from me."

"I got a cell signal about an hour ago, so I checked in with my mom and talked with Amanda. She said she hired someone to help with her workload at the studio. She and Leigh hired the same college student, so she must be helping at the theater, too."

"Leigh did mention needing to hire someone to do set design. It's a temp job, so it makes sense that they can share someone."

It felt good to talk about their hometown and the unaffected lives of those back home. Eli had dated Amanda Rivers since high school, although they had not made any official plans to marry. Leigh shared privately with Jeremy that she thought Amanda and Eli's relationship had peaked. They were drifting apart.

After dinner and a brief shower at the community bath house, Jeremy crawled into his bunk in the camper, away from the other men gathered by a campfire. He pulled out his phone to call Leigh. She answered in two rings.

"Hey," he teased, "remember me?"

"Oh, Jeremy! It's so good to hear your voice! Are you ok?"

"I'm fine. Just checking in to see how things are there. I've been missing you."

"It's quiet and lonely here at the house, although I did pick up a new employee who's doing an amazing job painting sets for the Christmas production."

"I heard. Eli's here with us. His dad and Mason are returning to Butlerdale, so he's bunking with me in Mason's RV. We're just glad he has a pickup truck." Jeremy paused. Should he share what he had witnessed this week?

"I've been following the storm recovery efforts on the news. It just looks terrible!"

"It's ten times worse than what you saw. It resembles a war zone. So many people have nothing left."

"Anything I can do to help?" Leigh felt suddenly trapped by her obligations. She would have gladly abandoned the theater if that would benefit the relief efforts.

"One of the things I have seen constantly is that there isn't enough food. Folks need non-perishable goods. You know, ready-to-eat stuff. The food that has come in so far is canned, and some of these people can't even find a can opener, let alone have a way to prepare it. Who can help organize a food drive? Eli's dad is coming back here in his box truck to bring some additional tools, tarps, that sort of thing. It would be great if he could transport whatever you can raise."

Leigh moved to her laptop as she began to type. "I'm on social media right now making an appeal, and I'll connect with Hank Jones and Uncle Mason in the morning to check their schedule. Don't worry. The downtown merchants have this covered."

"I love you."

"Love you, too. Be safe. See you by Thanksgiving?"

"I hope so. You know, we've got much to give thanks for. This week, I've been reminded how blessed we are to have access to the basic necessities."

After the conversation concluded, Jeremy laid back against his pillow, content he had finally heard Leigh's voice. His eyes were heavy, and he was asleep within minutes.

Chapter 9

A Community Reacts

God is our refuge and strength, an ever-present help in trouble. Psalm 46:1

The next morning, Leigh drove to the local wholesale grocer an hour before the business opened. T. J. Williamson immediately responded to her social media appeal. When she arrived, she discovered a parade of employees loading Hank Jones' box truck with Williamson Wholesale's entire inventory of individual packaged non-perishable food. Smiling, she spied T. J., pulling a pallet jack loaded with fruit cups. "Good morning, Leigh," he spoke in greeting. "I wanted to go with Jeremy, Mason, and Eli, but I didn't think I could keep up anymore." T. J. then patted his right knee, and Leigh realized the former marine master sergeant had discovered another way to serve. "I have enough on hand to probably fill half this truck. I can send one of my vans next week with more once I get a delivery from my main supplier."

"This is so great, T. J.," Leigh responded, offering a hug to a man she had known all her life, a man who refused to accept having his leg amputated after a devastating explosion in a desert ambush. Making up his mind in the field hospital, his grit, determination, and belief system allowed him to return to his hometown to grow a dying wholesale business into a thriving one. A family affair, his wife, Grace, and their three children were equally busy carrying cases into the truck. They were a fine-looking family, all with ebony hair and umber skin. It was Grace who pulled Leigh aside to convey an idea.

"Thanksgiving's right around the corner," Grace began, "and all I could think of last night is that so many tornado victims will spend the holiday either in a hotel room or a home that may or may not have electricity restored. I started praying about the situation..." She paused before blurting, "Do you think we could somehow deliver Thanksgiving to them?"

"What a wonderful idea!" Leigh beamed, embracing her. "Let's float the idea to the other merchants and see what we can do."

Grace and Leigh fanned out that week to visit the restaurants on the square. All of them offered assistance. Comparing notes a few days later, the pair met in Leigh's office.

"I can't believe we have an entire Thanksgiving dinner already promised," Grace scanned notes she had taken on her phone.

"It always seems our town has a great heart for helping others."

"So, how do we get this food five hours away? What's the plan?"

"Barney's Deli has some portable food warmers they use for catering. We can load them in a van or a box truck. Other caterers have said we could use their warmers, too."

"Great! We have several box trucks. T. J. and I can drive, but we can round up other drivers if needed. We'll need servers on the other side to prepare takeout containers."

"Count me, Abigail, Amanda, and Beth in. Jeremy says there are plenty of workers there who have volunteered to stay to help, too."

"We can get some college kids from CCF to individually package things like desserts, cranberry sauce, that sort of thing. I talked with the campus minister, who said they could do this as a last-minute project for any students still in town that Wednesday before Thanksgiving."

"First Christian has offered their gymnasium as a staging place. It's all arranged."

Grace looked at her friend and smiled. "Remember in our Bible study a few weeks ago how we discussed finding opportunities to serve? I prayed that God would give me something unique to do. Well, this is pretty unique!"

Chapter 10

Calls from Home

Fathers, do not exasperate your children; instead, bring them up in the training and instruction of the Lord.
Ephesians 6:4

Tristian offered to walk Lucy back to her dorm after the usual Thursday night gathering at Christian Campus Fellowship. She'd become a regular fixture there as she adored the music, camaraderie, and new friendships.

"I'm so glad you're coming to CCF," he said as they left the campus house.

"It's strange, but I feel really at home there." She tucked a wayward lock behind her ear. This was their first time alone, and while they had become friends, she was uneasy about saying something dumb and scaring him away.

"Yeah, I practically live there." They were walking along a tree-lined street, and he reached up to pull some acorns off a water oak tree. He absently threw them one at a time toward a wooden fence ahead of them.

Tristian grabbed more acorns from the next tree. "Where do you live?"

"Oh, I'm in Donaldson Hall on the front campus."

"Okay." Tristian ran out of oak trees and ammunition as they approached an intersection where the fence ended. Ahead of them was the Student Center. Tristian calculated the longest route possible to Lucy's dorm. They turned toward the biology and nursing buildings. Almost empty parking lots indicated that commuters without Friday classes had left the campus for the weekend.

"How long have you been going to CCF?" Lucy attempted small talk to fill the silence.

"Oh, since I was a freshman." Tristian put his hands inside his jacket pockets.

"Like me. What do you like the best about it?"

"I can be myself at CCF. Play what I want without being pressured, you know. I've been asked to play stuff for frat parties, but that's not my thing."

"That's not my thing, either," Lucy confessed. As soon as she said it, she felt embarrassed. She'd never been invited to any Greek life event. Why couldn't she make cohesive sentences?

A fraternity house down a side street hosted a cornhole tournament, and loud music blared from a portable sound system. The partiers were cheering and yelling at the fierce competition of the inebriated players. Suddenly protective, Tristian quickened his pace. He recognized some of these guys and knew they would give Lucy a hard time if they saw her.

"They're having a little too much fun, huh?"

Lucy agreed. "Aren't you glad we don't have drinking at CCF?"

Tristian laughed out loud. "That'd be a little contradictory, don't you think?"

Lucy chewed on her lip. Why couldn't she think of the things she wished she could tell Tristian? Here she was, finally alone with a guy she liked, and she kept saying boneheaded things. She had a billion thoughts, but her mouth could not form them. Arriving too soon at her place, Lucy and Tristian paused in front of the building.

"Thank you for walking me home."

"No worries. I don't live very far from here." Tristian cleared his throat before blurting his next statement, running his words together. "Say, I'm playing Sunday at Celebration Church downtown. I'd love for you to come with me."

"Um, sure. That would be great!"

The budding ministry temporarily met in Moon and Stars. Leigh had mentioned it in passing, but Lucy hadn't given it much thought until now.

"Cool. I'll give you a call Sunday. Maybe we can ride together?"

"I'd like that."

They stood there looking at each other as an uncomfortable silence settled between them. Neither one could figure out what to say or do next. In the distance, they could still hear the muffled beat of a rap song playing at the frat party. A siren blared, and suddenly the music ended. Lucy began climbing the steps toward the door.

When they reached the doorway, Tristian leaned in to kiss Lucy. Abruptly, a female student carrying an armload of textbooks burst through the doors, colliding with Lucy. Shrieking in surprise, Lucy tumbled down the steps as books pelted her.

"Hey, are you okay?"

Lucy had landed on her backpack, so no damage was done besides getting whacked in the head by a thick accounting textbook. It stunned her, but she finally spoke. "Yeah, I think so."

Tristian reached down to help her to her feet. He turned to the other student. "Hey, you need to watch where you're going."

Embarrassed, the student kept apologizing, explaining she was running late to meet a friend to study. Tristian helped the girl gather her belongings before she scurried away.

Tristan studied Lucy, looking for signs of trauma. "Are you sure you're alright? That was a big book that bonked you on the head."

Lucy felt a slight goose egg forming above her forehead. "I'm fine," she insisted, disappointed that heavy projectiles interrupted something special.

The moment ruined, Tristian ended the evening. "Good night. See you Sunday." Thrusting his hands inside his jacket, he descended the steps and headed toward his residence hall.

Upon arriving in her dorm room, she shut the door behind her and leaned against it. She closed her eyes and relived the moment when Tristian almost kissed her. Was she ready to move to a new level with him?

Head now pounding, Lucy sighed as she went to the bathroom to find some ibuprofen. Grabbing bottled water from the refrigerator, she drank several sips before noticing her phone ringing.

"Hello," she answered as she put the phone on speaker. Removing her jacket, she discovered a bruise on his her arm. It had already turned an angry purple.

"Lucy? Where have you been? I've been trying to reach you all day. Are you alright?"

It was Lucy's mother, Anna. "Hi Mom, yeah, I'm good. I was out with some friends."

"Oh, I'm glad you're becoming a little social butterfly again."

"So, what's up? Isn't it late for you to call?" Lucy took off her shoes and socks and found fuzzy slippers.

"I just hadn't heard from you today and was concerned."

Lucy decided not to disclose she'd just received a stunning blow to the head. Or that a boy she liked almost kissed her.

Anna continued her dialogue after Lucy said nothing. "Thanksgiving is almost here. I thought maybe I could come get you the weekend before."

Lucy noticed the use of the singular pronoun. "You're coming by yourself? Mom, you hate driving in Atlanta alone. Why isn't Dad coming?"

"Oh, he's got meetings at the home office in San Diego. He won't fly in until later that week." Lucy noted something strange about her mother's tone. She was trying too hard to keep things upbeat and optimistic. The conversation continued, one-sided, as Anna shared news from home. Lucy's headache raging, she began changing clothes as she readied for bed, half-listening. Satisfied to hear her daughter's voice, Anna wrapped up the call.

Lucy could not sleep that night. The over-the-counter medication had not done its job, and Lucy was miserable. Finally, she switched on her lamp, careful not to wake Claire. Finding the Bible the campus minister gave her on that first night at CCF, she flipped toward the poetry books in the middle, specifically looking for something she bookmarked from tonight's talk, a beautiful passage using allegory language comparing a deer's thirst to a human's quest for God. Finding Psalm 42, she whispered the words, allowing them to envelope her. A hunger formed as she flipped to the gospels and found Jesus for the first time, not as a character in a Christmas play who cooed and looked adorable while lying in a wooden food trough, but as a savior of her soul, the one who knew the confusion she was experiencing and was willing to help her deal with it. She wanted to know more.

The headache finally subsided, and she slipped into a shallow slumber, awakening at dawn. Sore from her fall, she shuffled her way into the shower. After dressing, she picked up her phone to call her father. There had to be some reason for this perplexing game her parents had now played for months.

"Hello, Lucy," Cory greeted in his usual way. "How's my girl this morning?"

"Hi, Dad. Do you have time to talk?" Lucy sat on her bed and brushed her hair.

He consulted his watch. "Yeah, I have a few minutes before I have a meeting. What's up?"

"Is there something going on? I talked with Mom last night, and she just didn't sound right."

"Oh, nothing is wrong. All is well." Cory quickly stated.

"Why aren't you coming with Mom to pick me up for Thanksgiving? You know how she flips out when she drives through Atlanta. Can't you change your travel plans?"

"She'll be fine," Cory assured. "I have things to do that day and can't turn loose. Do you want me to check with your grandmother to see if she will keep your mom company?"

"Grandma and Mom in Atlanta traffic? Dad, be reasonable."

"Hey, it's only a suggestion. Listen, don't worry about me and your mom. We're fine. How's classes going?"

She noticed the abrupt change in subject. "Good. I'm doing better in all of them. I might even make the Dean's list if I do well on my English lit final."

"That's great!" Cory turned pensive. "Hey, I'm so sorry again about not making that transfer a few weeks ago. I hope it didn't put you in a bind."

She didn't tell him about the incident in the Student Center. "It's good. Now that I'm making a little money working, maybe you don't have to worry about it."

"It won't happen again, I promise."

Lucy realized it was almost time for her bus. "Thanks, Dad. Gotta go. I'll talk to you later. Love you."

"Love you, too, princess."

She grabbed a juice box and an apple before rushing to the bus stop for downtown Butlerdale. Once she entered the bus, she found an empty seat and ate the apple. Thinking about her work, she was almost finished painting the Bedford Falls panels and was looking forward to creating the alternative reality town of Pottersville. Leigh seemed pleased with her work, and since Amanda had an out-of-town photo shoot, Lucy had gotten a lot done at the theater. Her deadline was looming immediately, but she thought she would make it.

Her phone buzzed, and she checked it. A text appeared.

"Lucy just called. She's figured out something's wrong. We gotta be more careful."

Cory wasn't the best at texting. And his mistake confirmed to his daughter that he and Anna were not "fine."

Chapter 11

A Meal on Wheels

My goal is that they may be encouraged in heart and united in love so they may have the full riches of complete understanding and know the mystery of God, namely, Christ. Colossians 2:2

The week before Thanksgiving, Butlerdale citizens anticipated the official start of the Christmas season. Municipal employees finished decorating trees on the square with abundant lights and décor that spread to the gazebo and other structures. On break from the university, Lucy arrived early and stayed late at the theater while she completed the set panels. When she and Leigh left each evening, they encountered workers testing the holiday lights, providing just the right ambiance to accompany the crackly feel of anticipation.

Leigh and Grace Williamson's dreams of providing a turkey meal with all the fixings came true, as T. J. Williamson involved another local merchant who ran a butcher shop. They smoked dozens of turkeys, and with the aid of all the downtown restaurateurs, donations began to converge at First Christian Church. Various tasks kept a steady stream of volunteers from area churches and the college ministries busy, and Grace oversaw the massive undertaking.

Lucy had already informed her parents about helping with the Thanksgiving meal, postponing her mother's trip to Butlerdale to mid-week. As she rode back to the campus house in the CCF van after packing supplies and nonperishable foods at the church, she called her mother. Unfortunately, the call went directly to voicemail. Phoning her father, she received the same result. Contemplating her next move, she decided if they couldn't physically talk with her, she would let them know she was onto them and their annoying secret-keeping.

I know everything isn't fine. What's wrong?

Sending the text to both parents, she awaited their response. It wasn't long before this message appeared from Anna.

We're good. Glad you're helping with the food project thing. See you Wednesday.

She texted back a screenshot of her father's text from earlier. *Explain this.*

Minutes passed before Cory shot back a reply. *Busted!*

Lucy was the first out the doors as the van parked beside the campus house. She walked to a brilliant yellow poplar tree that glowed in the evening sun. Trying her father again, he answered on the first ring.

"Lucy, we've tried to keep this under the radar for the past few months."

"What are you talking about, Dad? You and Mom's been acting strange ever since I got here."

"I'll confess! We've planned a family cruise for Christmas break. I got a great bonus, and we've made all the arrangements."

A cruise? Why such secrecy over a family trip?

"Where are we going?" Lucy pressed.

"That's the best part! We're heading to Cozumel! Your mother's been working out the details, but we finally got our passports this week. Hopefully, we still have time to work out the final details. Are you excited?"

Lucy was more confused than ever. "Um, we're going to Mexico?"

"That's right! You know your mother's always wanted to go! She's taking time off work so the two of you can do some shopping. I'll fly down to Miami, and we'll all get on that ship together!"

While this trip was the dream vacation Anna always yearned to take, Cory never wanted to go. They had countless arguments about spending this kind of money. Why was he suddenly on the Caribbean cruise bandwagon? Deciding not to challenge this about-face, Lucy turned on the faux charm. "This is wonderful, Dad! And you guys wanted to surprise me?"

After hanging up, Lucy stood under the poplar tree. She plucked a leaf off a branch to study its perfection. She had more questions than answers. Her father would never have agreed to such an extravagance unless something life-changing had happened.

"Hey," Tristian walked up, his face showing concern. "Anything wrong?"

"Oh, just talking with my dad," Lucy shared. She stopped short of explaining things that she didn't understand.

"Do you wanna catch a bite? I'm starved."

"Sounds good." The pair began walking across the parking lot. "Where do you want to go?"

"I think the Student Center's still open."

The same clerk who humiliated Lucy about her debit card stood at the counter. "I got this," Tristian offered. He chose a sub sandwich and chips, while Lucy ordered a garden salad with blackened chicken. After receiving their orders, they chose a small table near a window. The dining hall was almost empty. Plates and glasses clinked as they were being loaded into a commercial dishwasher. This was the last day of operations before the holiday, and the food service staff hurried to finish their shift. They all looked forward to a much-needed break.

"What time is your mom picking you up tomorrow?" Tristian asked between bites.

"Who knows? She said she's not going through Atlanta, so I'm guessing she's gonna get lost somewhere in north Georgia..."

Tristian chuckled. "I'm driving home after we finish packing food in the morning. We have a big family get-together on Thursday."

"That's good." Lucy munched on her salad, realizing she was hungry.

"Are you finished at the theater?"

"Yeah, I stayed late last night to finish the final panel. Leigh wants me to work for her after the break, designing some posters. Um, I'm kinda nervous about it. I've never done anything like that."

"You know, I took a design class last year. Maybe I can help. Um, that is, if you need it."

"I'd like that." She reached to touch his hand but turned over her glass of water, spilling it on both of them. There weren't enough napkins on their table to mop up the mess, so Lucy grabbed a handful from an adjacent table. "I'm so sorry. I'm always spilling things!"

Tristian blotted his shirt. "It's only water. No damage done!"

Mentally beating herself up, she knew her tentative attempt at affection failed miserably. Why couldn't she be assertive and confident instead of a bumbling klutz?

Their meal done, he walked her back to her dorm. Twilight colored the sky a brilliant orange as the temperatures dropped from the absence of clouds. As they strolled casually, Tristan jingled his keys and twirled them on his forefinger. Neither one said anything, and Lucy fretted over the silence but couldn't think of anything witty to say. Climbing up the steps, they paused outside the foyer.

"Do you want to get warm inside before you go?" Lucy offered.

"Yeah, that'd be great." Tristian opened the door for her.

Rubbing his hands together, he cupped them and blew on his chilled palms. Lucy turned toward her mailbox and unlocked it to check its contents. Finding nothing there, she secured it and returned to Tristian.

"Thank you for dinner," Lucy offered. "Um, sorry again for trying to drown you with my water."

Tristian tried again for a goodnight kiss. She didn't realize what was happening and turned slightly, and his lips grazed her nose. It startled her, and their noses bumped together. They both laughed in unison at their awkwardness before their eyes met. He pulled her into his arms and kissed her gently on the lips.

Chapter 12
Lying Eyes and Cloudy Skies

"For I know the plans I have for you," declares the Lord, *"plans to prosper you and not to harm you, plans to give you hope and a future."* Jeremiah 29:11

Claire and Lucy sat together on the concrete steps outside their building. A partly cloudy day before Thanksgiving, the afternoon warmth made them both sleepy. As predicted, Anna got lost twenty miles north of Butlerdale. She had corrected her steps and would drive up within a few minutes.

"I can't believe he got the nerve to kiss you!" Claire giggled at Lucy's recap of her first kiss with Tristian.

"Yeah, I'm still floating." Lucy hugged her knees, rocking back and forth as she relived the moment for the thousandth time.

"You have kissed a boy before, right?" The former Butler High School cheerleader teased. She had kissed lots of boys.

"Um, yes," Lucy's face turned beet red. "My last boyfriend and I dated for two years but broke up after graduation. He said I was 'baggage.'"

"Guys can be so mean!"

An SUV turned the corner, heading toward them, "At last! I told Tristian Mom might get here before Thursday."

She rose to gather a backpack and a duffel bag. "Bye, Claire. Have a good Thanksgiving."

"You, too," Claire waved as she walked toward her car. She would spend the holidays with local family.

Opening the hatch, Lucy slung her bags inside before hopping in the passenger seat. "Hi, Mom!"

"Sorry I'm late." She kissed the air near Lucy's cheek. "Who was the girl sitting with you?"

"Oh, that's my roommate, Claire. She kept me company while I waited."

Anna looked puzzled. "I thought your roommate's name was Ali."

Lucy shook her head in disbelief.

They drove north, then east across the state. It took an hour longer, but finally, familiar landmarks began to appear. Lucy didn't realize how much she missed her hometown. Arriving at the modest middle-class, split-level home, Lucy and Anna carried her light luggage into the house. "Where's Dad?"

"Oh, I'm not expecting him until much later. He's been working so hard lately so that he can be off next month."

Inside her childhood bedroom, Lucy unpacked. She brought home clothes with the intention of returning with heavier ones for winter. While sitting on her bed, she noticed the room was recently painted. All her posters and pictures from high school had been taken down, and the room seemed more like a guest room. A sign of the times. She had moved out, after all. Leaving the bedroom, Lucy observed that the entire house had been painted, and the usual clutter no longer existed. New flooring made rooms seem larger. Was her mother going through a mid-life crisis?

Curious, she entered her father's office. It still existed in its original form, with his University of Georgia diploma proudly displayed, football prints on each wall depicting Georgia Bulldogs' triumphs, brown leather furniture, and an antique barrister bookcase. She sat in the office chair behind his desk, turned on a lamp, and began to snoop.

Upon first inspection, nothing indicated anything amiss. She thumbed through a small stack of papers related to his work with medical equipment, but nothing stood out. Opening the center drawer of his desk, she hit paydirt. Inside were a series of pamphlets, all relating to cancer. The one labeled "You've received a diagnosis...what's next?" had an appointment card attached, with her father's name written in red ink. He was scheduled to visit this specialist in a week. Her heart began pounding in her throat. This made complete sense! Tears burning her eyes, she read the flyer to understand his type of cancer. While the literature was written with an optimistic slant, she felt pending doom. The treatment only prolonged the inevitable.

Lucy couldn't breathe. She felt the walls closing in on her. Shutting the drawer so she couldn't see his name on the card, she rose only to knock over the table lamp, shooting the bulb. She fumbled with the lamp to upright it. Rushing outside, she found her bicycle in the garage and pedaled hard to a corner park. She needed to clear her head to think.

Once there, she parked the bike next to a covered pavilion. Going inside, she sat on a picnic bench. Swirling images cluttered her mind, and she couldn't shake the knowledge that her father was suffering from a terminal illness. A small, still voice whispered in her head – she knew what to do. "Um, God, are you there? Uh, this is Lucy. Lucy Grant. If you can hear me, help my dad. I know we don't go to church and stuff, but I've been going to CCF, so that should count for something. Can you make him better? I promise..." Uncontrollable sobs interrupted her prayer. She sat with her face in her hands for several minutes, weeping. Finally realizing she needed to get her act together, she wiped her face with her sleeve. Her parents did not need to see her like this. Hopping on her bike, she rode around the neighborhood until she gained sufficient composure to return home.

Anna and Lucy worked in the kitchen that evening, preparing sides and desserts for Thanksgiving Day. Lucy's specialty was pumpkin pie, as she had made this recipe since she learned how as a teenager. She blended a creamy pumpkin layer using a hand mixer before pouring it into a prepared graham cracker crust. They shared small talk, but mostly, Lucy kept quiet. There was no sense in bringing up her discovery, and she had decided to try to make this the best Thanksgiving they had ever had.

After dressing in cotton pajamas, Lucy curled up on the sofa and discovered "Now, Voyager" on a streaming channel. Sharing popcorn with Anna, the pair watched one of Leigh's favorite movies and discovered Bette Davis, the iconic Hollywood star, in one of her most memorable roles.

Cory arrived sometime after midnight. He had missed a connecting flight and was rerouted to Chicago before landing in Atlanta. Hushed whispers of her parents awakened Lucy's slumber on the couch, and she rose to greet him, rubbing the sleep from her eyes.

"Hey, princess," he exclaimed brightly despite a haggard appearance, pulling his daughter into his embrace. Clinging to him, she hugged him a little harder than usual.

"What's this? Do I detect you've missed me just a little?"

"Oh, Dad. I didn't realize how much."

Anna hung up his slightly damp overcoat in the foyer closet. "Is it raining, Cory?"

"A little, but it's supposed to be pretty for Thanksgiving." He turned to his daughter, who now stood next to him. "I'm going to take a shower and go to bed. We have the entire weekend to catch up!"

The next morning, Lucy and Anna worked on roasting a turkey in the oven. Reading a recipe a friend had shared, Anna insisted that Lucy prepare the bird while she worked on the dressing. "It says here to remove the turkey from its brine bath and pat dry."

Taking the poultry from a bowl in the refrigerator, Lucy transferred it to a roasting pan. Slippery, it shot out of her grasp to land unceremoniously upon the tile floor. "Oops!"

As her mother laughed, Lucy scooped up the bird and looked for signs of damage. "What does it say to do now?" She held the bird underneath its wings.

"Since dropping it on the floor isn't part of the instructions, put it underneath running water and make sure it's clean. We'll put him in the oven before anything else happens!"

Cory and his brothers had an early tee time, and by the time they finished a round of golf, they arrived just in time for a succulent turkey to emerge from the oven. "Mmm," he exclaimed while walking through the kitchen. "Lunch smells great!"

Eager to lavish praise, Anna responded after kissing her husband on the cheek. "Your daughter is turning into quite the chef!"

Gazing in appreciation at the holiday spread, Cory grinned. "If anyone leaves today hungry, there's something wrong with their taste buds!"

The house filled by noon. Lucy's grandparents, uncles, aunts, and cousins gathered around the dining room and kitchen tables. After her grandfather offered the blessing, the hungry horde filled their plates and ate with gusto. Sitting with her cousins, Lucy had no appetite. All the preparation had turned her stomach. At the first opportune moment, she slipped out of the house to walk around the neighborhood.

The weather front that produced rain at midnight had come through, leaving cooler air and a slight breeze. Wearing a jacket, Lucy pulled the hood over her head as she walked with the wind behind her. All she could smell was roasted turkey! She didn't have time to shower before their guests arrived, and she imagined she reeked of poultry. Returning to the gazebo she visited the day before, she perched again at a picnic table.

"What are you doing out here?" Turning, Lucy discovered Grandma Ellie. "Everyone was raving about your pie just now."

"Oh, I needed to get some fresh air." Lucy didn't make eye contact. She concentrated instead on some pecans she had picked up from a nearby tree. She kept stacking them up and knocking them over.

Grandma Ellie observed more than Lucy thought. "You just picked at your food. What's the matter?"

Her grandmother's soothing voice struck a chord. "Something's going on with Mom and Dad. Dad's sick. I think he has cancer."

Grandma Ellie decided it was time to tell her granddaughter the entire truth. "Yes, they found out right after you left for college. Your mom went into denial and renovated the house. Your dad acts like it's nothing major."

"And this trip they're planning? To Cozumel? It must be pretty serious if we're going there."

Grandma Ellie placed her hand on Lucy's. "There's no trip to Mexico. It's a ruse to stop you from asking them what's wrong."

Lucy stood with anger burning in her eyes. "Why such an elaborate lie?"

"They didn't want you to worry. Your dad's going to Houston for surgery at MD Anderson Cancer Center. That's where he's been this week, meeting the doctors and care team who will be in charge of his case."

"Why are you telling me all this?"

"They're keeping this from you because they didn't want to upset you. His first symptoms happened the week after you started college. They thought he could start treatment and get things under control before you found out. As it turns out, he may be out there for several weeks, beginning when you're having finals. Your mother said the last place you need to celebrate Christmas is with them in a hospital room."

"It's not going to be the same. I need to be out there with them."

"I know you want to be there, but they're right. You can stay with us if you'd like."

That evening, Lucy finished cleaning up the house with Anna. All their company had left, and Cory was watching a football game. "Mom," she asked while putting table linens in the washer. "I know about Dad."

Anna's face drained of all color. "What did you just say?"

"Mom, I know, and it's okay."

Anna and Lucy embraced as they shared mutual tears. No further words were said.

Chapter 13
An Unexpected Reunion

Enter his gates with thanksgiving and his courts with praise; give thanks to him and praise his name. For the Lord is good and his love endures forever; his faithfulness continues through all generations. Psalm 100:4-5

Jeremy noticed residual oranges and yellows of fall clung to trees along the roadside as he drove toward home. He had been gone a month as he assisted those in the storm-ravaged communities in Alabama. As he formulated a plan to surprise Leigh on Thanksgiving Day, he visited a car rental agency, where he told the manager that he didn't care what they had to offer; he just needed wheels. He was fortunate to leave the parking lot in a four-wheel drive Jeep.

As he drove across the state toward Georgia, his mind drifted to his many obligations with work. As things began to calm down in Alabama, he spent some evenings following up with sub-contractors on his construction projects. All of them were on schedule except one, which was the job he hoped would be completed before Christmas. Unfortunately, the owner fired the bricklayer, and the roofing company put the wrong shingles on the house. So, if he did not accomplish anything else during the Thanksgiving holiday weekend, it would be to put out fires.

His mind turned to Leigh. He missed her. He couldn't wait to see his beautiful wife, feel her in his embrace, touch her skin, and run his hands through fiery hair that always smelled like a subtle spring rain. When they last spoke, she seemed confident about meeting deadlines for the Christmas musical that would premiere next weekend. She was happy that she had hired the college student to help with the sets, alleviating some of the stress of final preparations.

During his free time, he read about the hormone therapy the specialist prescribed. He still didn't understand how it all worked but tried to learn more for her sake. It just seemed complicated. If it was successful and Leigh became pregnant, would she be able to carry a baby to term? After weeks in Alabama, he witnessed countless children who relied on their parents for survival. Did he have it in him to be a good father?

Once he crossed the state line, he left the interstate to meet the major highway that led to Butlerdale. In twenty minutes, he had crossed the square as he headed toward the outskirts of town, where he would cross Salem Creek on his final approach to the gingerbread-trimmed farmhouse. Several vehicles in the yard indicated they had company, his in-laws, and extended family. Pulling next to the house, he unfolded himself from the Jeep's confines, stretched, and realized Mick, their five-year-old beagle, already detected his presence. The hound greeted his master with a wagging tail and hearty barking, and Jeremy petted his four-legged friend.

A loud, running chainsaw distracted him. Why would anyone want to cut down a tree on Thanksgiving Day? That was when Mick disappeared along with the familiar farmhouse scene, and Jeremy found himself again in his usual bunk in Mason's RV. His mind snatching to retrieve the dream, his demeanor turned to downheartedness when he realized he was still in Alabama and the machinery running was Eli tuning a fickle motor.

It was the evening before Thanksgiving, and they had spent the day closing the command center, a final assignment, before returning to their families. FEMA personnel had finished assigning their trademark single-wide travel trailers to those who required them. Jeremy was grateful things were winding down since many work crews had already left the area.

The remaining volunteers would remain an additional day as they assembled at the elementary school early Thanksgiving morning to coordinate the significant undertaking of the community Thanksgiving meal from Butlerdale. While Jeremy, still smarting from his tantalizing dream, knew that finishing this job was now mere hours away as he and Eli rode toward the school to meet with those assembled there. Mason Young had ridden with T. J. Williamson from Butlerdale, and half a dozen box trucks lined up in front of the school. Mason offered a heartfelt prayer of gratefulness before teams spread out to begin the food distribution.

Everyone wore food service gloves as they filled to-go plates with turkey, mashed potatoes, green beans, cranberry sauce, and yeast rolls. The assembly line approach worked well. To keep things efficient, beverages were assembled in another traffic lane and desserts in another.

Grace Williamson noticed a bearded man whom she suddenly recognized. Wide-eyed, she hugged Jeremy. "Hey, it's so good to see you!"

"Thank you for helping Leigh with this project. I'm glad we're doing this."

Many local volunteers wanted to assist, so there was quite a crowd to help with the distribution. Cars began lining up at nine o'clock to pick up the meals. Jeremy put on an orange vest as he began directing traffic, where recipients drove up to request a specific number of boxed lunches. Within the first hour, hundreds of meals passed into automobiles occupied by grateful storm victims. Crews also fanned out into nearby neighborhoods to deliver meals to those unable to trek. No food remained by lunchtime, and the group began to disband.

At that instant, Jeremy noticed a trio of redheads removing their security vests. His heart skipped a beat when he realized Leigh and her cousins had been distributing beverages at the far end of the school campus. How did they manage to slip by him? Leigh looked up and recognized the bewhiskered, curly-haired man staring at her. No words were spoken. She ran toward him, and as they met, he picked her up, spinning her around and around in his arms as he hugged and kissed her.

"I wanted to surprise you," she professed.

"You certainly did that."

"I'm not sure how I feel about your beard." She felt his newly-grown whiskers. "Hm, I might let you keep it."

"As you wish," he laughed.

By then, Eli and Amanda had found each other and had a similar reunion, and the two young couples walked back to the school gym and began cleaning up. Even though none of them had eaten a bite, it was a Thanksgiving Day that they would always cherish.

After retrieving his gear at the campground, Jeremy rode home with Leigh while Beth remained behind to ride with her father in the RV after they broke camp. So happy to be in the presence of his wife, Jeremy teased her all the way home, and she reciprocated, knowing he always chose this mechanism to cope with leaving her for any extended period.

Their beagle, Mick, barked and wagged his tail as Jeremy and Leigh greeted him that evening. Stopping to pet the friendly pup, Jeremy played a quick game of ball with his four-legged friend before he and Leigh stepped inside the farmhouse.

"Do you want any dinner?" Leigh asked as they entered the kitchen and switched on the lights.

"All I need is you," he responded, pulling her against him.

Leigh's parents hosted Thanksgiving dinner that evening. Leigh and Jeremy arrived an hour late...

Chapter 14
Maternal Advice

*"Blessed is she who has believed that the
Lord would fulfill his promises to her!" Luke
1:45*

Leigh visited her mother the morning after Thanksgiving.
Discovering Caroline raking oak leaves in the backyard of the log
cabin where she and Leigh's father, Sam, resided, Leigh grabbed a
garden rake to share the labor.

"Mom! Why aren't you using that electric blower we bought Dad for Father's Day?" Leigh was perplexed at her mother's unnecessary work.

Caroline chuckled as she stopped to lean against the gardening tool. "Maybe we should have a second one, just for me. Your dad ran the battery down earlier today when he blew off the driveway."

The pair worked for about an hour, exchanging pleasantries, a never-ending, comfortable conversation between mother and daughter. In her mid-fifties, Caroline worked professionally as a registered nurse. Agile and fit, she and Sam had downsized after Leigh and Jeremy married. The cabin had been a labor of love, their dream home, designed to their specifications by a talented son-in-law.

Once finished with yardwork, Caroline invited Leigh inside to share coffee. They settled together in a cozy breakfast room lighted by the morning sun.

"Mom, I need to discuss something with you." Pausing to stir her coffee, Leigh sighed. "We want to try again to have a baby. Dr. Freed prescribed hormone therapy a few weeks ago."

"How do they make you feel?"

"Moody. Ill-tempered."

"Well, that explains a lot." Caroline's face twisted with humor.

"Thanks, Mom." Leigh rolled her eyes.

"Leigh, you almost died! It scared me to death when you had your miscarriage."

"It's a risk I'm willing to take." Leigh's green eyes glistened with fixed determination.

"Your Aunt Eileen suffered from the same thing." Sam's great-aunt never had children of her own.

Leigh exhaled. "I don't want to hear about Aunt Eileen. I've heard it all before."

"I'm just reminding you it could be hereditary."

"Have you ever wanted something so badly that you would do whatever it took to help make it happen?"

Caroline's face provided the answer. They both knew the sacrifices made during Leigh's childhood as Caroline pursued a nursing degree and began a career as an emergency room nurse, caring for critical care patients. There were weeks that Caroline caught glimpses of her teenage daughter, straining their relationship. The breaking point was a stormy night when Leigh, Abigail, and Amanda arrived as victims of a car crash. After patiently assessing their wounds, Caroline realized none had life-threatening injuries. Although the wreck was not Abigail's fault as the driver, it was the wake-up call that Caroline needed. She turned in her resignation within the week and took a position as a pediatric nurse at a private practice.

Being a mother is one of the best things that ever happened to me," Caroline admitted. "When I look at you, all grown up, married to a wonderful man, and running a successful business, my heart is full. I only want the best for you."

"Thanks, Mom."

Caroline's Bible sat on the table. Picking it up, she flipped to the first chapter of Luke's gospel. "God performed several miracles to enable Mary to bear His Son. It started with Elizabeth and Zechariah, a childless couple past their prime who found themselves expecting a marvelous surprise. Their son, John, became that voice in the wilderness who prepared the way for Jesus and His ministry. An angel also appeared to Mary, giving her explicit instructions and comfort. Instead of making excuses and wanting out of the arrangement, she accepted her role as the Messiah's mother with grace, dignity, and full surrender. And God also knew that she would need Joseph's full support. It was a far-fetched story for him to believe, but after an angelic being explained the situation, his love never wavered. He was all in."

"Every night, I pray for a God-sized miracle," Leigh disclosed.

"I don't think a night has passed since you were born that I didn't pray for you and your wellbeing. There's always been a dialogue between me and Jesus about you. Listen, if God can give an old, childless couple a child who has peculiar eating habits and little fashion sense, then He knows what's best for you and Jeremy. It all takes great patience to wait."

Leigh exhaled. "Waiting has never been my best virtue."

"If you're serious about becoming a mother, you must learn to control your impatience. Believe me; you'll get plenty of practice."

Chapter 15

A Christmas Play

"For I know the plans I have for you," declares the Lord, "plans to prosper you and not to harm you, plans to give you hope and a future." Jeremiah 29:11

Opening night for "It's a Wonderful Life" buzzed with energy, and the attendees for the premiere were excited to attend the event. Leigh and Jeremy stood in the foyer, greeting local theater lovers, their closest friends, and family. For this special presentation, Leigh asked Beth to play Christmas music on the theater's concert grand piano. Beth chose a variety of genres, from timeless classics to carols to pop and contemporary Christian. It set the tone for the play based on the classic Jimmy Stewart movie.

Brisk sales that evening and the presale tickets available weeks in advance sold out the auditorium. For the next two hours, the audience became immersed in the classic tale of a desperate man who thought the world could live without him and his guardian angel, who showed him his life was worth much more than he ever dreamed. The professional acting ensemble portraying various characters brought the story to life. Still, as Leigh and Jeremy watched from their private balcony, they decided that Lucy's stunning artistry set this production apart from the ones they had presented over the past few years.

Leigh gave opening night tickets to Lucy for her friends, so Tristian, Claire, Tate, and others from CCF occupied a cluster of orchestra tickets. Lucy beamed that they all could attend that Friday night. Following the show, the play's producer approached her. "We've asked Leigh Day for the sets you designed," Arthur LeBlanc explained. "The production continues through the last week in December, and this will save so much time with sets in other cities."

Lucy blushed. She didn't realize her designs had made an impact.

"I want you to know you did a good job. You have great potential."

She looked at Tristian and Claire, then back at Mr. LeBlanc. "I don't know what to say. Um, thank you."

After arriving at her dorm that night, she and Claire sat on their beds, talking. They were still wired from their evening's adventures.

"I noticed Mr. LeBlanc and Leigh studying the sets last week. He said I had great potential. Do you think he really meant it?"

"He wouldn't have said it if he didn't mean it." Claire shared her roommate's elation. She turned to another matter. "Um, so, like what's going on with you and Tristian? He can't take his eyes off you. Has he kissed you again?"

Lucy stammered, "Um, we're just friends."

"He told Tate he had pretty strong feelings about you."

Lucy's face brightened. "Oh, we're just talking."

"You'll be going out next."

Lucy stretched and yawned. "I'm a little tired, so I think I'll turn in. I want to get a good night's sleep before my finals in the morning."

The next day after classes, Lucy walked to the campus ministry house. It was her new norm to visit there to unwind. She enjoyed hanging out with her friends, enjoying trivia, and attending a beginner's Bible study. Tristian was playing acoustic guitar when she walked in.

"Hi, Tristian," she greeted, approaching the stage where he sat on a wooden bar stool.

"Hey," his smile indicated he was glad to see her. "You finished with classes?"

Tucking her hair behind an ear, she sat a backpack in a chair. "Yeah. I'm done with finals."

"What are you doing, um, for Christmas?"

Lucy turned her head. "I think I'm staying with my grandparents. My parents are going to be out of town."

"For the holidays? That's like crazy."

Lucy burst into tears.

"Oh, I didn't mean that. Uh, don't cry." Tristian unstrapped the guitar and placed it on a floor stand.

"It's okay. You don't know what's going on. My dad's going to Texas to have cancer surgery, and he's gotta be in isolation or something. They think I shouldn't go out there."

Tristian embraced her. She buried her face into his Butler U sweatshirt. As he held her, Tristian had an epiphany. "Listen, uh, my family is skiing for Christmas in North Carolina. My parents have a cabin rented, and there's always plenty of room. If it's okay with my folks, would you like to spend the holiday with us?"

Lucy sniffled. "That sounds nice. Are you sure you want me there?"

"Yeah. I'll call my mom to see if it's okay. You'll love my folks. Oh, and my sister, Katy."

He pulled out his phone and made the call.

Chapter 16
A Discovery

So we fix our eyes not on what is seen, but on what is unseen, since what is seen is temporary, but what is unseen is eternal. 2 Corinthians 4:18

Following the "It's a Wonderful Life" weekend at Moon and Stars, the play set the stage for holiday shows and performances throughout December, from high school choral concerts to the university string orchestra, with presentations practically every evening. Leigh thrived in this setting, as each day offered new challenges and adventures, and she faced them all with an unruffled attitude.

It was the week before Christmas that she finally remembered the Fontanini™ nativity. The professional cleaning crew that took care of keeping Moon and Stars sparkling clean was vacuuming her office, and while they were doing so, Leigh took the box to her car as she left for the afternoon. While she and Jeremy had put up their Christmas tree and outside greenery and lights, she had forgotten this addition to their home décor and planned to assemble it that evening.

Driving down Magnolia Avenue toward home, Leigh felt familiar cramps. Her heart fell into her stomach. She wasn't pregnant. Accelerating through town, she ran a traffic signal. Immediately, flashing blue lights and a siren caught her attention. Pulling into a parking lot near the university, she sat there, awaiting an officer to approach. She rolled down her window.

"Are you in a hurry to get somewhere? Did you not see that red light?" The young officer questioned.

"I'm sorry," she stammered as she studied him. He was a new hire to the police force, and Leigh didn't recognize him.

"I'll need to see your license and proof of insurance."

Handing over these cards, she watched him walk to his squad car, where he remained for several minutes. When he came back, he gave her the ticket he had processed. "You need to be careful. Have a good day."

Still furious about the ticket when she arrived home, she grabbed her purse and the box and slammed her car door as she stomped into the kitchen, where she flung these items on the table. After changing clothes, she returned to the kitchen to focus on the nativity set. She saw the gouge and rip on the top of the box for the first time. Inspecting the box, she sliced the packing tape with a knife and carried it to the family room. Unpacking the stable, she set it on top of a cabinet. Each character was individually boxed, so she unwrapped them and placed them inside. And then she discovered that one character was missing.

Where was baby Jesus? Rifling through the packing material, she found a loose sheep in the outer carton. Tearing through tissue paper and cardboard, she ripped through the individual boxes, feeling under the flaps to ensure he wasn't caught under them. Not finding him, she backtracked to the car and moved the seat back to establish he hadn't fallen out there.

Cursing, she remembered the day the nativity set arrived and who delivered it. Overwhelmed by anger, now focused on the ever-careless Hugo Barnes, she picked up her phone to call his office to complain. A recording gave her options, and when she selected "customer service," she ended up in a continuous loop of merry holiday music and a recorded voice that stated her call was important and that someone would answer shortly. Infuriated, she swore with renewed intensity as she threw the phone across the room.

The cell phone landed at Jeremy's feet as he entered the house. Witnessing Leigh's fury, he picked it up and retreated to the carport. He wondered what he had done now, mentally making a list of any grievances that could cause the woman he married to hurl objects and use scorching language. He heard Christmas music and discovered the looping recording. Even though the phone was damaged, it still worked. He ended the call and reentered the house.

Leigh sat crumpled on the floor, crying hysterically.

"What's the matter?"

"There's no baby Jesus," she tried to explain through her sobs, although what she said was unintelligible, and all Jeremy understood were the words "no baby."

Jumping to conclusions, his worst nightmare unfolding, he couldn't believe their misfortune. "Oh, Leigh, I'm so sorry."

Leigh changed the subject abruptly. "What's wrong with me? Why can't I get pregnant like everybody else?"

He consoled her by taking her into his arms. "It's all right," he muttered, stroking her hair.

She pulled away from him, not wanting his sympathy. "I don't understand why you've stayed with me this long. I can't give you a baby. Maybe you need to find someone else who can give you everything."

"Nah, I'm used to you. Besides, no one else would put up with you throwing a phone at them."

"That's not funny. I didn't hit you!"

He saw the scattered packing material covering the family room floor. "What's going on here? What's got you so riled up?"

"There's not enough time before Christmas," she mumbled as she considered ordering a replacement. "I've missed my chance."

He softly shushed her. "We don't have a Christmas deadline for a baby like Mary and Joseph. Honest."

"What are you talking about?" She stopped crying as she stared at him.

"Losing another baby. You just said there's no baby." He looked so earnest, so concerned.

She laughed. It felt good to laugh, and she suddenly realized the humor in the entire situation. Pointing to the nativity scene, she explained. "I said there's no baby Jesus. He's missing from the box."

Chapter 17
A Slight Moral Dilemma

Create in me a pure heart, O God, and renew a steadfast spirit within me. Do not cast me from your presence or take your Holy Spirit from me. Restore to me the joy of your salvation and grant me a willing spirit, to sustain me. Psalm 51:10-12

The following day, Leigh took the time to search for the missing figurine. The cleaning crew had arrived to clean after the previous night's presentation of the classic Barbara Stanwick movie, "Christmas in Connecticut."

Catching Walt, the janitorial service owner, she interrupted him as he vacuumed the lobby. Covered in tattoos, the former prison guard had traded a dangerous job in Atlanta to serve various Butlerdale businesses with his quality cleaning services.

"Walt, can I ask you a question."

Switching off the vacuum cleaner, he responded. "Sure. What can I do for you?"

"I'm missing a baby. Have you seen it?"

Taken aback at her statement, his gaze dropped to her belly. "I'm sorry, I, um, didn't know you had a baby."

"Oh, no, not a real child. A little one." She measured with her fingers. "He's part of a Christmas nativity set."

The custodian still looked confused. "Where did you have it last?"

"In my office. Y'all were cleaning in there when I left yesterday."

"No, I don't recall seeing it. If I find it, I'll let you know."

Leigh returned to her office and started looking again. The doorbell jingled as Lucy walked in and saw Leigh underneath her desk.

Startled by the ringer, Leigh raised up in the tight space and conked her head. "Ouch!" Rubbing her head, she peered above the desk to see who entered.

"Um, are you okay?"

"Oh, hi, Lucy," she responded as she turned off a flashlight. Standing and straightening her clothing, she turned toward her. "You haven't by chance seen a baby Jesus figurine? It's part of the nativity set I ordered, and he's not in the box. He may have fallen out here, but I can't find him anywhere. I'm beginning to think he may not have been in the box in the first place."

Lucy heard blood rushing in her ears. She knew where the figurine was and began to grasp that the miracle baby she found on campus belonged to someone she knew. She hesitated. "Um, I've not seen it around here," Lucy finally stated.

"I know it sounds silly, but the whole point of the nativity is having a baby Jesus as the centerpiece."

"Well, maybe you'll find it." Lucy turned away to go into her small studio. She had been working on the promotional posters for January events, and once Leigh approved the designs, she would upload and order poster-sized prints for the lobby.

Leigh followed her into the workroom, where she examined Lucy's artwork. "These are exactly what I had in mind," she exclaimed as she flipped through Lucy's printed samples. "I'm glad you could take the time from your work with Amanda to finish these before Christmas. I'd like to have them up when we host the holiday movie marathon beginning tonight."

"I checked the schedule with the printers, and they promised they would have them ready by the end of the day if I sent the files before lunchtime." As much as she enjoyed Leigh's company, Lucy now felt antsy. "I can pick them up later if you would like."

"No, I'll have to pay, so I'll pick them up." Leigh paused, and that was when Lucy noticed that she was holding an envelope in her hand. "I would just like to thank you so much for sharing your talents with us. Jeremy and I appreciate you and hope you have a merry Christmas." The gift came with a heartfelt embrace.

Later, as she sat in her dorm room, Lucy stared at the check. It was so much more than she ever expected. Initially shocked about the figurine, Lucy knew she needed to let Leigh know she had the missing baby Jesus. Nevertheless, she considered it an amulet, as every positive thing that had happened lately went back to that fateful day when she saw it fall out of the delivery truck.

Claire entered the room after she and Tate finished delivering baked goods from the campus house to the university's fire department. Later, the couple, plus Tristan and Lucy, planned an evening out to visit botanical gardens renowned for their unique holiday light displays. Claire would spend the remainder of the holidays with her father and aunt. Lucy's parents were still in Houston, where Cory was in isolation, so they agreed that Lucy needed to accept the invitation to spend Christmas with Tristian's family.

"Claire, I have a question for you. Do you believe in good luck charms?"

Removing her jacket, Claire sat down on her bed, facing Lucy. "I don't really believe in good luck," she admitted while pulling her long hair into a ponytail. "I think God allows good to happen without any sort of trinket. Why are you asking?"

She held out the figure in her open palm. "This is really weird, but I found this in the street the day we met."

Claire took it. She admired baby Jesus in all his sleepy glory. "He's a cute little guy," she admitted before returning it to her roommate.

"I know who it belongs to, but I just can't quite give him up. I'm afraid if I do, my luck will run out." She paused as she considered her next admission, something she had been careful not to share. "Claire, my father has cancer. He's out in Texas getting treatment. Since they need to keep him isolated, I'm going to spend Christmas with Tristian and his family."

"Why haven't you told me this before?" Claire began shaking a bottle of polish to touch up her nails.

"I don't know. Ever since I've been here, they've acted weird. When I was home on Thanksgiving break, I discovered their secret."

Shaking her head, Claire began to fit the puzzle together. "I wondered what was up with your parents but didn't want to pry."

"I'm sorry I hadn't told you." Lucy stood to slip a sweater over her head.

"Is your Dad going to be okay?" Claire asked as she blew on her fingernails to help them dry.

"I think so. Dad's surgery went well, and he's taking chemo." Lucy's face brightened.

"So, are you going to return the figurine?"

"Should I? I literally found Jesus that day."

"You found Jesus because I invited you to CCF. It was exactly what you needed. And Tristian was so glad I invited you. He said you were the cutest girl there that night."

"Thank you for being my friend," Lucy admitted, her eyes welling in tears.

"You know, I picked you because I couldn't take any more of Ali's perfume, either!" There was a small craft bag sitting on Claire's desk. "If you decide to return Baby Jesus, you'll need something to put him in!"

Collecting the sack, Lucy returned to her desk. She needed to compose a quick thank-you note.

That night, as the two couples began their drive out of town, Lucy asked Tristian to detour their route to travel down Salem Church Road. It was not out of the way, and as they enjoyed local Christmas lights, they passed the historic church and its namesake creek before Lucy asked to stop at a farmhouse. She hopped out of the car to run to the porch to hang a present on the front door knob. Claire grinned from the backseat as she realized Lucy had taken her advice.

Chapter 18

A Christmas Eve to Remember

Or suppose a woman has ten silver coins and loses one. Doesn't she light a lamp, sweep the house and search carefully until she finds it? And when she finds it, she calls her friends and neighbors together and says, "Rejoice with me; I have found my lost coin." In the same way, I tell you, there is rejoicing in the presence of the angels of God over one sinner who repents. Luke 15:8-10

It was late evening when Jeremy and Leigh returned home from hosting the holiday movie marathon. Exhausted from the long day, they entered the home through the side door, and within a few minutes, they were already asleep. Neither of them had seen Lucy's package, and it remained where she left it all night.

The next morning, Christmas Eve, Leigh rose at her usual early hour, cozy in flannel pajamas and sitting at the kitchen table reading the story of Jesus' birth from the gospel of Luke. When Jeremy shuffled in, clad in pajama bottoms and a T-shirt, he sat adjacent to Leigh after pouring a fresh mug of coffee. "Morning," he announced, leaning in to kiss her.

Looking up from the Bible, she had just finished the passage. "Good morning, sleepyhead," she responded in her usual sunny tone. It never got old, their familiar rituals.

"I thought I'd do breakfast this morning," Jeremy offered, sitting down his mug. "What would you like?"

"Before I answer, did you hone newfound cooking skills while camping in Alabama?" Leigh teased, a lilt to her voice.

"Of course. I'm ready for my own cooking show! So, what will it be, milady?" He rose from the table, grabbed a kitchen towel then bowed dramatically.

She laughed. "I almost want to sell tickets for this. Why don't you surprise me?"

Soon, the tantalizing smell of bacon filled the kitchen as Jeremy worked on cheese grits and scrambled eggs. Leigh took time to prepare fruit and wheat toast, and soon, they were enjoying a scrumptious breakfast for two. "What do we have planned for today?" She asked as she picked up a piece of crisp bacon.

"I was thinking about finishing up a little Christmas shopping today, you know, hit the stores with all the other last-minute shoppers. It's always fascinating to watch folks who waited until the last minute to make their purchases." He paused to wink. "So, no apologies for whatever ends up under the tree, right?"

"I'm a little worried."

"What about you? Want to go out on an adventure of monumental proportions?" He wiggled his eyebrows before grinning with mischievousness.

"Actually, Mom wanted me to come over to help her finish some baking. And I have some cooking to do as well. You could drop me by her house on your way into town." She paused. "I'm sorry about this week and how emotional I was earlier about the nativity scene. I just felt so sure after doing the new therapy that we would deliver good news this Christmas." Her voice trailed off.

He covered her hand with his. "It's okay. We just have to be patient a little while longer."

Finished with his meal, he rose from the table as he remembered something. "I meant to check the front porch last night. There should be some packages there that were delivered yesterday. The backorder for your dad's gift should finally be here."

"Maybe there's something for me out there?"

"Nah. I had my eye on a Christmas sweater at Target that lighted up and played music. It should be on clearance by now."

"You wouldn't..."

"I'm telling you, if they still have it, you'll see it under the tree!"

Jeremy opened the front door and found the packages sitting neatly on a woven rug. He noticed a brown craft gift bag hanging onto the door knob. It had a small tag with his wife's name on it.

"Hey," he exclaimed as he juggled the boxes and the bag. "Someone must have stopped by last night. There's a present here for you."

She was distracted by clearing the table and loading the dishwasher, so she said, "Just set it there on the counter. I'll open it later."

Packing a suitcase for her trip, Lucy paused to consider the number of outfits she would need. Knowing she was heading for a colder altitude, she would leave some lighter-weight clothing in her dorm room. Ultimately, she decided on several sweaters and jeans and threw in a dress she had worn one Sunday morning when Tristian was playing at Celebration Church. He had commented that he liked the floral-shirred waist A-line dress, especially since she had paired it with knee-high leather boots. She noticed he couldn't keep his eyes off her that afternoon as they enjoyed a walk around the square.

She purchased gifts for Tristian's family, mostly gift cards for his parents and sister, although she had bought a devotional book and some guitar-related items for Tristian. As she was wrapping his gifts, her phone rang, and absently, she answered it.

"Lucy? It's Grandma Ellie."

Taken aback by her grandmother's call, Lucy responded with a loving tone. "Merry Christmas, Grandma. I hope you and Grandpa are doing well."

"Have you talked with your parents today?"

"No," Lucy's heart sank. News from Houston from her grandmother instead of her parents?

"Your father's going to be fine. Your mother said it wasn't as bad as they originally thought. The isolation ends a few days before New Year's!"

There was a long pause. Lucy's voice quivered. "Oh, thank God."

"Your mother's phone was acting up, so she wanted me to call you. She's going today to get a new phone."

Lucy laughed. "It's about time she got a new one."

Grandma Ellie changed the subject. "Your mom said your boyfriend asked you to spend Christmas with his family."

"Yes, I met him a few months ago at a campus fellowship group."

Grandma Ellie interrupted. "What sort of group?"

"It's a Christian campus thing. I really like going to it. I've spent a lot of time there this semester."

"It's always bothered me that your parents never took you to church. I've heard of campus ministries, and I'm glad you're making friends."

"Thank you, Grandma. I appreciate your support. If you are worried about my going off with my boyfriend and his family, please don't. His parents are a very nice couple and are all very much involved in their church. The cabin where we are staying has several bedrooms, and I will have my own room. Um, his mother wanted to make sure I was comfortable with the living arrangements, so I will be in a room next to the master bedroom on the main floor. Tristan and his sister, Katy, will be in loft rooms on the second floor."

"I like how his mother thinks." Grandma Ellie relaxed. "So, tell me about Tristian. Is he good-looking? What's his major?"

"He has curly brown hair, and he wears it shoulder length. He's taller than me. He's probably Grandpa's height. At CCF, he plays guitar in the praise band and helps lead Bible study. His major is music, but his minor is in chemistry."

"He sounds great. Please send me some pictures."

"Sure. Um, are you mad that I'm not coming home for the holidays?"

"We'll miss you, but we all understand. You're young. Be young! We may ride over to Butlerdale after the holidays for a quick visit."

"That's great. I have a couple of work-related items the first week of January, but my hours are flexible at my jobs."

"Jobs? You have more than one?"

"Yes, I'm, um, like a photographer's assistant, and I also do design work for the local theater. I'm staying really busy with work, school, and campus ministry."

"Wow, that's super! I'm so impressed! Listen, your parents told me how to transfer money to your checking account. You're going to need some spending money. I wasn't sure what I would get you for Christmas, but that'll have to do. Make sure to buy something cute to wear on the slopes!"

"Oh, thank you, Grandma! And thanks for the good news. I love you so much! Merry Christmas!"

Chapter 19

A Brown Paper Package

In the beginning was the Word, and the Word was with God, and the Word was God. He was with God in the beginning. Through him all things were made; without him nothing was made that has been made. In him was life, and that life was the light of all mankind. The light shines in the darkness, and the darkness has not overcome it. John 1:1-5

On the holiest night of the year, Leigh and Jeremy attended an evening Christmas candlelight service at Salem Christian Church.

While she and Jeremy usually worshipped downtown at First Christian, she was drawn to the small country church where generations of her family served. She felt at home as she sat with her mother and father while singing traditional carols and hymns. It was here where she started her Christian journey years ago through the witness of the great aunt who once occupied the Mitchell homestead, revealing Jesus and his plan of salvation. That was the beginning of a revival for her family and their involvement. Now, her parents stayed busy as volunteers for a congregation known for benevolence and kindness. Those in attendance lighted candles at the end of the ceremony, and the gathering sang "Silent Night," before departing for their homes and family gatherings. After the service, the two couples crowded into a booth at the Waffle House on the main highway, where they enjoyed a late dinner as Christmas carols played on the jukebox amid a parade of townspeople who shared this annual tradition.

Upon returning home, Leigh finally picked up the brown paper bag left on the front door the previous night. Inside, she extracted an envelope and a tiny wrapped box. Opening the card, she admired artwork that she suddenly realized was homemade, as the artist rendered a pen and ink depiction of the holy family surrounded by shepherds, sheep, and a glowing angel. Inside, a handwritten message stated the following:

Dear Leigh,

Thank you so much for everything.

Thank you a million times for the job. I love working for you and Amanda, and I'm glad I can continue to work for you guys in the new year.

One morning, while heading to art class, I saw something fall from a delivery truck as it pulled away from my dorm. I put it in my pocket to keep it from getting run over by a car. I have considered it my lucky charm, for finding baby Jesus that day was also when I first went to CCF. Something is changing in my life, and I'm glad. Maybe this little guy will bring you the same joy.

Merry Christmas,

With love, Lucy

Tearing off the wrapping paper and tape, Leigh opened the small box to reveal the missing character in her nativity scene. He had come full circle, and grateful tears ran down her cheeks as she took him to the foyer, where she placed baby Jesus in front of Mary and Joseph in the stable.

Chapter 20

A New Year

Even youths grow tired and weary, and young men stumble and fall; but those who hope in the Lord will renew their strength. They will soar on wings like eagles; they will run and not grow weary; they will walk and not be faint. Isaiah 40:30-31

The new year brought fresh opportunities and ministries in Jeremy and Leigh's hectic lives. Jeremy began a new project building a retirement neighborhood for senior adults, as his work crews and subcontractors finished all the houses he had designed that year, just in time for many of the families to move in during the last week of Christmas vacation. Leigh met with Arthur LeBlanc to secure the schedule of plays for the entire year. As promised, Leigh held a job for Lucy to do the set designs. Meanwhile, Leigh also inked a formal lease agreement with Compassion Church to hold weekly Sunday morning services there.

After the Epiphany, January 6, the traditional date that the wise men found and worshipped the newborn king, Leigh carefully packed the nativity scene and stored it along with the rest of her Christmas ornaments and décor. Holding the much-traveled baby Jesus, she thought again about how it affected a lonely college student who needed to hear the good news of Jesus. It was funny how, after December 25, a replacement showed up that Jeremy had ordered, although lackadaisical delivery driver Hugo Barnes managed to deliver it across the square at Magnolia Studios. Leigh decided to pack the newcomer since she had something special in mind for the original one. She would hold onto it until the next yuletide season, when she would return it to the person who took such care in preserving it from harm.

Encouraging news from Athens indicated that Cory's surgery was a resounding success, and he would return to work, albeit remotely, while his immune system regained its strength. He would continue chemotherapy treatments for the next year at MD Anderson, but his case manager assured him these were precautionary. A grateful Lucy shared her father's prognosis with her friends.

Dr. Freed decided the second week in January to change tactics again, realizing that the mixture of hormones needed tweaking.

Leigh began a new cocktail of injections. As an immediate result, an emotional rollercoaster fueled her existence. It did not help that Jeremy's new project consumed his time; even at home, he was on the phone most evenings until bedtime. Everything culminated one morning when she hurled the fertility calendar at him in a rage. It was, ironically, Valentine's Day.

"Whoa, honey!" Jeremy exclaimed as he swatted the calendar away from him. "What did I do to deserve your wrath?"

"It's your fault we're in this predicament!" Leigh snapped. "You can't stay home long enough for this therapy to work!"

"Why are you blaming me? Look! I brought you roses!" He pointed to a stunning bouquet of red roses on their kitchen table.

"Okay..."

He moved closer, still cautious of flying objects. "And concert tickets..." He fanned them out in his hand.

She folded her arms and glared at him. "Keep talking."

"And we have reservations for the weekend in Chattanooga. That bed and breakfast place you thought looked interesting the last time we were there. You know, the one overlooking the Tennessee River?"

"Do you promise to stay off your phone and focus on us?"

Sighing, he pulled her into his arms. "I'll try."

Away from home, obligations, and distractions, the couple spent a well-earned and relaxing weekend off, enjoying each other's companionship as they visited the aquarium, strolled through Rock City, and took a late-night carriage ride after dining at a popular riverside restaurant. Their cell phones were turned off, all calls went to voicemail, and texts and emails had to wait.

As soon as they returned to Butlerdale, individual commitments began to occupy their lives, and it was not until the first week in April that Leigh realized that she had missed her monthly cycle. Mindful that the hormones may have caused this, she visited Dr. Freed's office for advice, even admitting to the physician that she had stopped using the calendar to track critical days. She didn't tell him she weaponized it when she was upset with Jeremy. When a nurse came into the examination room wearing an unreadable expression, she handed test results to the physician, who good-naturedly delivered the patient's prognosis.

Stunned, Leigh left the doctor's office numb and speechless. On a gorgeous spring day for their weekly luncheon, Abigail and Beth awaited her on the square as Amanda and Lucy were on a recon mission at the country club in preparation for the Butler High prom. Jeremy delivered take-out Chinese as a surprise, and their conversations centered around Abigail's discussion of spring concerts on the square and Beth as she detailed a recent reunion with her ex-husband, Rick. Watching Jeremy as he teased Beth, Leigh decided it was not the time to reveal the information to her husband. After lunch, Leigh visited with Beth at her studio, where she blurted to her cousin the news she could no longer contain.

Leigh packed a picnic for their evening meal as she and Jeremy strolled to Grahame's Pond, a picturesque lake on the edge of their property. On this day, spring pastels reflected in the glassy waters from flowering azaleas lining the well-traveled path. An old fishing cabin once stood on the shore, but Jeremy had dismantled it after it had fallen into disrepair. With only the rock chimney remaining, Jeremy designed a small covered pavilion around this focal point, and their family often used it as a gathering place.

After dinner, they shared a hammock that faced serene waters. Resting her head against his shoulder, they lay there quietly as tree frogs and crickets began a nightly serenade.

"I have something to tell you."

"Hmm," he responded with a monosyllable.

"Lately, I've been daydreaming about our future. I have Lucy now working at the theater, and Tristian has been invaluable in helping on busy evenings. It's the right time for us to go to the next level."

Assuming she was talking about Moon and Stars, he kissed her forehead. "Are you thinking about adding more shows?"

"Not exactly. I want to reduce my work hours to fix up one of the spare bedrooms."

Confused, Jeremy responded. "I have professionals that can do that work. I've seen you paint. It's not your best skill."

"There are other things I need to do. It'll be November before we know it."

"What happens in November?"

"That's when our baby is due."

"Our what?" Excited, Jeremy rose from the hammock, causing it to twist, and the couple tumbled out of it onto the soft grass below. Laughing as his wife landed on him, Jeremy kissed Leigh while wiping happy tears from her cheeks.

As Hannah in the book of 1 Samuel dedicated her firstborn to the Lord, so did Leigh as the months inched toward autumn. She promised God this precious child would grow up in a loving home where worshipping Jesus would always take priority. As Dr. Freed considered this an at-risk pregnancy, he took extra care to ensure Leigh carried the fetus to full term and assured her he would deliver the baby. However, as her due date approached and passed, Leigh began to wonder if her prayers for pregnancy were too specific and that the child had taken up indefinite residence in her uterus.

On Thanksgiving morning, intense back spasms awakened Leigh. She rolled over to wake her snoring husband.

"Jeremy, wake up. It's time."

Half asleep, he mumbled, "Time for what? We don't have to go to your parents until noon."

Rising from the bed, she doubled over in acute agony. She reached over and shook him. "Jeremy, wake up! You gotta take me to the hospital unless you wanna deliver a baby!"

"Now?" He looked confused.

"Now! I'm in labor!"

Leigh and Jeremy arrived at the local hospital, where a reduced emergency room staff met them at the car with a wheelchair and rolled the soon-to-be mother to a triage area. Jeremy explained their special circumstances and asked that they contact Dr. Freed. Since he had doctor's privileges at the facility, Dr. Freed left his family and made the hour's drive to Butlerdale. Wearing a "First Annual WKRP Turkey Drop with Les Nessman" T-shirt, the quirky obstetrician entered the birthing center and found the couple in their assigned labor room.

"Happy Thanksgiving!" He shook Jeremy's hand before examining the patient.

"How far apart are the contractions?" Dr. Freed asked the nurse assigned to them.

"They're coming every four minutes."

Leigh looked worried. She had suffered through false labor pains for two weeks, and they were nothing like these now rippling through her body. She moaned in anguish.

Dr. Freed took her hand. "Listen to me. You need to relax. Remember the Lamaze classes you took? Just take deep, cleansing breaths."

"I don't know if I can do this," she confessed. "Maybe I need to rethink having a C-section."

"I'm not going to leave you alone, and neither is Jeremy. We're going to stay with you. Just breathe."

Ethan Mitchell Day debuted after Leigh suffered through hours and hours of labor. The wee one voiced a quavering cry as he tested his lungs for the first time. Exhausted from her efforts, Leigh cried tears of joy as Dr. Freed placed Ethan in her arms. Hearing his mother's soothing voice, baby Ethan calmed down as Leigh held him against her bare skin. She whispered to him (and God) a gratitude prayer for his safe delivery.

Excited about the birth of his son, Jeremy bounced out of the room to announce to their friends and family in the waiting room, "It's a boy!" No one had the heart to explain to the ecstatic first-time father that they all knew the newborn was a boy because of the gender reveal the couple had months ago.

Epilogue

Though you have not seen him, you love him; and even though you do not see him now, you believe in him and are filled with an inexpressible and glorious joy! 1 Peter 1:8

A couple of weeks following Ethan's birth, Leigh's uncle and aunt, Mason and Jessica Young, stopped by the farmhouse for a visit.

"He's beautiful," Jessica exclaimed while holding the infant. With wispy black hair and dark eyes, Ethan favored his father.

"Thank you, Aunt Jess."

"Have you talked with Beth lately?" Jessica asked while making faces. Ethan yawned and stretched while holding Jessica's thumb.

"She and Rick visited the hospital the day after Ethan's birth, but I've not spoken to her since. It's been so busy here that I hardly have time to talk with friends." Leigh pushed her hair out of her eyes. Her bangs were in need of a trim.

"Did you know they're expecting twins?"

"Twins? Oh, wow! When did she find out?"

"This week. Beth had an ultrasound, and they discovered two heartbeats!"

"That's amazing! She'll be a great mom!" Leigh paused in thought. "What about Solstice? She told me they had added more concerts." After the rock group reunited the previous summer, they had taken on a twenty-five-city tour across the United States.

"Beth assured me that New Year's Eve will be the last night she'll perform for a long time. She already has a slight baby bump!"

Mason cleared his throat. "Leigh, we wanted to ask you something."

"Sure," Leigh took Ethan from her aunt and laid him in a bassinet. Ethan relaxed and closed his eyes. It was nap time.

"We're going to host a live nativity at First Christian." Mason paused to look at his wife. "We usually have a baby doll to stand in for Jesus, but we thought this year might be neat to have a live baby."

Leigh narrowed her gaze while gently rocking the bassinet. "And you want Ethan to play the part?"

"We would love for you, Jeremy and Ethan to play the holy family."

The tabletop nativity scene sat on a cabinet in the family room, and Leigh glanced at it. Realizing the implications of this unexpected invitation, she smiled. God's promises continued to amaze and sustain her.

As Leigh sat in the stable on Christmas Eve with Jeremy, she held Ethan in her arms. Initially, the babe voiced his displeasure at lying in the manger, so she picked him up to keep him calm. She wondered if Mary did the same thing with Jesus, knowing the straw in the manger would irritate the newborn just as it did over two thousand years later to another miracle baby. As a cow mooed and a donkey brayed, their modern-day staging drew a steady stream of visitors on that chilly, moonlit night. Mason narrated the Christmas story while the church choir sang carols. Various parishioners played the parts of shepherds, angels, and magi.

When the evening came to a close, Jeremy whispered to his wife. "Did you ever dream when we couldn't find the baby Jesus for your nativity set that we'd play the part a year later?"

Leigh looked down at Ethan's contented face. He had fallen asleep. Smiling, she handed the sleeping infant to Jeremy. "With God, nothing is impossible."

Acknowledgments

First and foremost...*Thanks be to God for his indescribable gift!* 2 Corinthians 9:15

It's my sophomore book, and I am very humbled by those who have taken the time to read my debut novel, *Summer Solstice*. Unlike the first volume, *Finding Baby Jesus* did not take forty years of wandering through the wilderness of my mind!

The genesis for *Finding Baby Jesus* came quite by accident. Neil and I were newlyweds, and I wanted to decorate according to my individual tastes and style. I ordered a basic Fontanini™ nativity set. My sister, Lesia, received one when she first married, and I liked the tradition of adding to it each year. When the package arrived, I set it aside because it was October. Weeks later, when decorating the house for Christmas, I unpacked the carton to set it up on my dining room buffet. There was a stable, an angel, some sheep, a shepherd, Mary, Joseph...but guess what? I didn't have the main character! When I inspected the box, there was a gouge in the side, just big enough for Baby Jesus to escape.

Even though I ordered a replacement that arrived just a few days later, I realized if I lost Baby Jesus, someone surely must have found him! And from that humble beginning, an allegory tale began weaving itself. Writing a novella about a lost figurine has been quite challenging! I pray you discovered the magic of Christmas miracles as you read this story.

None of this would be possible without the love and encouragement of my husband, Neil. Always supportive, Neil has my best interests at heart. Please pray for him and his continued patience with me...he has endured many evenings when I have read aloud to him!

A very special thanks goes to my editor, Rebecca McClendon MacArthur. She was unafraid to tell me what didn't work in the original draft and helped me develop new ideas. Rebecca has a great husband in her corner, Tom MacArthur, who provided valuable tech support!

The stunning artistry of Natalie Orbeck continues to amaze me! The cover art and inside illustrations are exactly what I had in mind. Thank you, Natalie, for understanding the vision!

To my family...my brother, Tim, and my sisters, Lesia and Patricia. Our parents instilled the importance of Christmas, family, and how to share the love of Jesus with others. We continue their legacy. To my wonderful in-laws, Glenn, Paul, and Molly, thank you for your love and support. We enjoy being Uncle Neil and Aunt Lynn to all the nephews and nieces!

To my wonderful friends, Donna, Kristi, Sheila, Maria, Melanie, Michele, Rhonda, and Cathy. To paraphrase the author, John Donne, "No woman is an island." Each of these women of God has shown me what it means to follow Jesus, no matter where the road leads. I am a better person knowing them!

And finally, my deepest gratitude goes to the staff and congregation of Tabernacle Baptist Church, where I have recently celebrated my thirtieth anniversary. It is joy unspeakable to serve such a wonderful community of believers!

About the Author

Lynn Crawford Weathington enjoys writing, traveling, music, and photography. A technical school graduate with a degree in Secretarial Science (back when you could get a degree like that), Lynn has served in church administration most of her adult life. Her debut novel, *Summer Solstice*, was a 2023 Georgia Author of the Year award nominee for Best First Novel. An American Christian Fiction Writers member, she lives in Carrollton, Georgia, with her husband, Neil.

lynnweathingtonbooks.com

Made in the USA
Columbia, SC
26 October 2024

44683869R00072